THE

GIFT

Dr. John Meade

Prelude

892-832 B.C., Northern Kingdom of Israel

The king of Israel was clearly agitated and the members of his court were wise enough to remain silent. Looking at his officials and military officers he boiled over in hot displeasure shouting,

Where is he? Where is the man of God? What is his delay?

The man in question was Elisha, a prophet of the Most-High God and for the record, he was not beholding to anyone--not even kings, and especially those that kept one foot firmly planted in darkness. Yet whether conditions are light or dark, God sends His servants wherever and whenever He pleases.

The fact that the king expected the prophet was largely due to Elisha's own actions. Or was it God's? On two previous occasions, the man whose miraculous ministry was to exceed that of his mentor Elijah, had forewarned Israel's monarch of invading Syrian raiders-even citing the precise location of their attacks. With a score of two to zero, he had a perfect track record befitting those who bear the prophetic mantle. For anyone daring to speak for God with anything less than flawless accuracy would invite swift and certain retribution.

Despite the bald reformer's insistent message of repentance and a return to Jehovah, the land was flush with pagan practices and a people who found it easier to trust in themselves--except when danger threatened their lives! Eventually Elisha, whose name meant *God is salvation,* would minister in the Northern Kingdom for sixty years during the reigns of four different sovereigns.

But there is more going on in the narrative.

Apart from the heightened anxiety of Israel's ruler, another king was also keenly interested in the whereabouts of Elisha. In fact, the king of Syria's concern may have been more pressing than that of his rival. Assembling his servants and court officials, he continued the pattern of kings by expressing his frustration with a strident demand,

Will you not show me which of us is for the king of Israel?

It was a reasonable request. How could anyone know the plans of the king spoken in his private chambers unless there had been a traitor in their ranks? But the king was dealing with a spiritual dimension that he knew nothing about. He did not know that God ruled in the affairs of men and that every human heart lay open before Him. The supernatural was natural to Israel's God and this truth applied to His servants.

Those surrounding royalty are typically chosen for their wisdom and fidelity. Drawing upon a reserve of courage, one official broke the weighty silence with an explanation,

It is not us my lord. It is Elisha, the prophet who is in Israel, and he tells the king of Israel even the words you speak in the privacy of your bedroom.

The fact that it was God Almighty who empowered Elisha to listen in on his plans went right over the head of the king. Angrily he commanded,

Go out and find him so I can send troops to seize him.

It was later reported that Elisha was at Dothan located some twelve miles north of Samaria, the Northern Kingdom's capital. A march from Damascus would require four to five days under good conditions. And so, with horses and chariots an army was sent out to capture a man of God--and admittedly, one who heard the secret plans of his enemies.

What was the king thinking? Could the prophet's ears be open to this new plot as well?

But kings will be kings, dictators will be dictators. And God, well...He remains Sovereign over all things in heaven and on earth.

Chapter 1

1979, Sant'Angelo di Brolo, Sicily

By every description it was a beautiful, bright sunny morning in the little Sicilian town of Sant'Angelo di Brolo. Located sixty kilometers west of Messina it was nestled among the hills of the Nebrodi mountain range at an elevation slightly over 1,000 feet.

Its population was close to 4,000 souls which did not include the smaller pockets of residents that sprinkled the surrounding region. One such smattering included a husband and wife, a grandmother or *nonna* in Italian, and three small children; the oldest of which was a little girl celebrating her sixth birthday.

As a special treat and with her mother's permission, Nonna Grazia, pronounced GRAH-zee-uh, decided to take her granddaughter into town. Although she practiced spreading love among all three of her grandchildren, Nonna Grazia had a special place in her heart towards the big brown-eyed girl who, in so many ways, reminded her of herself.

Despite her young age, Michelina was sharp as a tack and she never stopped asking questions.

Nonna what are those bright lights in the sky? Why is the moon so round? Why does the sun go to bed at night? Why do you cut your roses that way…?

Unceasing but always intuitive!

Then there was the matter of their dispositions. Grandmother and granddaughter were a pair, each demonstrating strong, unyielding and at times simply defiant wills. They both possessed a gritty character that welcomed truth but gave no quarter to those who didn't share their convictions. Finally, and despite the difference in years, each framed life in terms that were either white or black. No room at all for gray!

*****

Nonna Grazia, when are we leaving for town?

With a smile the older woman replied, *just a minute child, we'll leave as soon as I'm ready.*

Wrapping her shawl around her shoulders, Nonna Grazia took Michelina's hand into her own and started down the semi-paved road to the town. After a twenty-minute walk, they reached the town piazza which was already bustling with activity.

Wide-eyed, Michelina observed vendors setting up booths filled with fruits and vegetables, shop keepers readying their stores, older men sipping caffé's on outdoor tables, and most importantly, she spied her favorite gelateria!

Oh Nonna, can we please stop at the gelateria? After all, it is my birthday and I'm sure you would like some gelato too! In fact, I'll help you pick out a great flavor!

With a small chuckle, the girl's grandmother surrendered to the inevitable.

Of course, child for that is why we came to town today. Your birthday deserves a proper celebration and I'm certain gelato will help to do that!

With an ear to ear smile, Michelina replied, *thank you Nonna-- and I love you, even if we don't get gelato!*

I know Michelina. I know. Now come along.

*****

The gelato was divine and there was simply no way that granddaughter and grandmother could avoid a second round. The dense, smooth, creamy texture and rich flavors did much to create a special day for a special child.

But there was more.

Before getting up from their table, Nonna Grazia caught the gaze of a man she had never met but had heard plenty about. He was a traveling *evangelista* who would occasionally pass through the region preaching to whoever would listen to him. His actions did not sit well with the local parish priests who warned their congregants to avoid him and his teachings.

And now he was coming straight to their table.

Quickly turning to her granddaughter Grazia said, *Come along Michelina. I need to get you home to your parents.*

But by then it was too late.

Buon Giorno!

Please signora, if you can spare a moment I have something to say to you about this little girl sitting beside you.

Somewhat annoyed by the intrusion, Grazia responded, *Signore, non ti conosco. I do not know you and I need to get my granddaughter back home to her parents.*

Signora, he replied, *I mean no harm and in fact when I first saw you and your granddaughter I did not think to come over to you. But then, the Spirit of God turned me aside to give you a message concerning this little girl.*

Though shocked at the entirely unexpected nature of the encounter, Nonna Grazia was strangely drawn to the dancing flames of fire that filled the man's eyes. His face was kind, his demeanor humble and despite her anxiety she relented.

Say what you must say Signore.

Nodding his head in thanks, he then turned to Michelina who had been sitting quietly while listening to every word.

Little girl, God Almighty has His hand upon you and His love surrounds you. He has marked you for good and He has chosen you to be one who will serve Him. You will see and hear things that others will not see nor hear. Your gift will make a way for you to go before great men.

Quickly turning to Nonna Grazia, the man added,

Remember well what was spoken today and pray dear woman for God's will to be done in this child's life. She will have an important mission and her gifting will affect many people.

And without another word, the servant of God walked away, never to be seen in Sant'Angelo di Brolo or that region again.

Nonna! Who was that man and can we go home now? I want to go home and play.

Of course, Michelina. Of course! Let's get started.

The old woman had much to think about and the man's words seemed to have penetrated right into her soul. Marked for good, chosen, and a gift of seeing and hearing what others could not see or hear. It was almost more than what she could handle. But Nonna Grazia was indeed a praying woman; a practice her granddaughter would later acquire as well.

Although what had taken place was outside of Grazia's normal experience, she made a commitment to bring the man's words back to the Throne Room she so often visited herself.

Chapter 2

Tough neighborhoods!

By any reasonable standard Planet Earth in the twenty-first century was not a safe place. The Korean Peninsula was an armed camp with the added volatility of a nuclear-tipped Northern regime led by its notoriously unpredictable dictator.

The Chinese, having adopted capitalism as a pragmatic means to fund their ambitions, cast aside international criticism to dredge out strategically important islands in the South China Sea five hundred miles from the mainland. According to one high ranking official who chose to remain unnamed, China's growing influence in the region was becoming *exceptionally menacing*.

But that was not all.

The Russians, who according to a segment of the U.S. population, had given the current president the 2016 election, were also back in the Middle East, peddling their influence while propping up the bloody Assad regime in Syria. The Russian bear, though considerably downsized from its Soviet years, still had its claws, powerful jaws, and ambitions! It seemed that wherever the U.S. had a strategic interest, the Russians made sure they played on the other team.

However, the perennial global hot spot was really a tiny sliver of a country that was home to over six million Jews, slightly less than two million Arabs, and several hundred thousand *others*. As the Middle East's only true democracy, it attracted the hatred of its neighbors like bees to honey. Since its birth as a nation in 1948, the Jews had fought seven official wars as well as seven additional conflicts each requiring a significant military response.

For the surrounding Arab nations, losing a conflict to their Israeli enemies was shameful but also recoverable. Yet the Jewish State had to continually win for in defeat they would lose everything. Moderate states such as Egypt and Jordan could get along with Israel but others such as Iran constantly plotted its destruction—and that was a real problem!

The Iranians, wanting to extend their influence and brand of religious extremism throughout the entire region, could not get past the Jewish issue. Given their geography, it was the six-sided burr in their saddle they couldn't do much about. Still they recruited surrogates such as Hezbollah and Hamas and armed them to the teeth with rockets and high-tech weapons.

But the desired weapon of choice had been put on hold--and most sane people wanted it to stay that way including Israeli's prime minister who claimed that eighty percent of his nation's security threats emanated from the Islamic Republic of Iran. Strengthening his argument, Israel's leader went on to label

Iran as *the greatest generator of terrorism in the world* with plans to destabilize the region and annihilate the Jewish State.

Not exactly comforting words from a country run by a tyrannical group of religious extremists!

And if the shaking of countries and regions were not enough, domestic issues in America revealed deep fissures among a people whose pledge read *one Nation under God, indivisible, with liberty and justice for all.* Accusations and mistrust separated countrymen and the elected president found himself under persistent attack before serving his first year in office. The god of political correctness threatened in a way once thought impossible, to redefine traditional views of good and evil, the acceptable and the unacceptable.

Yet there was hope, for God never leaves man without words to steady his ship and to light the way forward. Centuries before, the prophet Haggai penned the words of a heavenly voice saying,

Yet once more I shake not only the earth, but the heavens.

Haggai went on to explain that the shaking was for the removal of those things which needed to be removed so that the things which could not be shaken would remain.

And so, earth shook at the command of the Lord.

Chapter 3

Moreover, the word of the Lord came to me, saying, 'Jeremiah what do you see?' And I said, 'I see a branch of an almond tree.' Then the Lord said to me, 'You have seen well for I am ready to perform My word.'

Jeremiah 1:11-12

1979, Sant'Angelo di Brolo, Sicily

Months after Michelina met the strange *evangelista* in her town's piazza she had the first of many unique experiences which she would later describe as *a knowing*. Recognizing the hand of providence upon her granddaughter, Nonna Grazia would often share with Michelina her thoughts about God and the Bible. Although she did not fully understand the implications of the child's *marking*, she was wise enough to realize that she would need much prayer and encouragement as God's plan unfolded.

One day as Michelina was finishing her chores in the family's general store or *negozio,* an image flashed across her mind of her uncle Angelo who lived more than an hour away in the city of Messina. Her uncle was a frail older man and she saw him lose his balance on a ladder and fall to the ground where he lay motionless. Although she barely knew her uncle, the graphic image so startled her that she ran out of the store and across the street to Nonna Grazia's house. Throwing open the front door, Michelina raced inside frantically looking for her grandmother.

Nonna! Nonna! Something terrible has happened to Uncle Angelo. Nonna where are you?

Tears filled the young girl's eyes as she remembered seeing the shock on her uncle's face as he fell backwards off the ladder. Coming in from the terrazzo, Grazia put down her watering can and scooped her clearly distraught granddaughter into her arms. After a long patient hug, she asked,

Tell me Michelina. Why are you so upset child?

A tumble of words followed as Michelina labored to describe an event that was so foreign to her.

Nonna, I was sweeping the floor in the negozio and thinking about what I would do once I had finished. And then like a motion picture I saw Uncle Angelo climb a ladder on the side of his house. He tried taking another step up the ladder but he lost his balance and fell. I saw him hit the ground and not move.

Nonna what can this mean? Did something really happen to Uncle Angelo or is it my imagination?

For several minutes Grazia sat quietly beside her granddaughter. Her thoughts were drawn to the words of the *evengelista*.

Little girl, God Almighty has His hand upon you and His love will always surround you. He has marked you for good and He has chosen you to be one who will serve Him. You will see and hear things that others will not see or hear. Your gift will make a way for you to go before great men.

As she rehearsed the words one phrase stood out and began repeating itself: *You will see and hear things that others will not see or hear! You will see…you will see…you will see!*

At last, she spoke to her granddaughter and said,

Michelina, I do not know why you saw Uncle Angelo fall or if something really happened to him. But what I do know child is that whenever something like this happens we should pray and ask God that everything would be alright.

*****

Later that evening the family received a brief telephone call from Uncle Angelo's wife Maria. She explained that earlier in the day she found Uncle Angelo lying unconscious near his ladder. With the help of their oldest son Tony, they rushed him to the closest hospital where the doctor on duty admitted him for a possible concussion but otherwise all his vital signs were good.

Before leaving the hospital, the attending physician told Maria that her husband was either a very lucky man or somebody had been praying for him! In his medical practice, the type of fall that Uncle Angelo experienced would have almost certainly resulted in a severe injury or even death.

Before turning in for bed that night, Nonna Grazia slowly rehearsed the day's extraordinary events. There was no possible human explanation for Michelina being able to see what she saw, miles away from the accident, and in such vivid detail. Also, what she witnessed sparked an outburst of earnest prayers for Uncle Angelo's wellbeing. His doctor even accepted that prayer could have been instrumental in preventing more serious injury.

Remarkably, the prophetic words of the *evangelista* for her granddaughter seemed to have come alive! Uncle Angelo and his family directly benefited from Michelina's gift and she was certain there would be many others as well.

Suddenly feeling her age, Grazia decided to call it a night and go to sleep. Climbing into her bed, the old woman turned off the lamp and whispered a quiet prayer in the darkened room.

Oh God of heaven thank you for saving Uncle Angelo from serious injury and I ask that he recover quickly. I also thank You for marking my granddaughter with Your unfailing love and gifting.

A little smile emerged on what once was a beautiful face.

And God, although it's unlikely I will be around to see it, I want to praise You for the great plans You have for that child.

Moments later, Nonna Grazia fell fast asleep as angels stood by protecting one of God's favorite daughters.

Chapter 4

June 1980, Departing for the States

Michelina's father had decided!

The family would sell the *negozio,* their home, and whatever else they were not able to squeeze into their luggage for the Alitalia flight from Rome to New York City's Kennedy International Airport. Husband and wife both had relatives on Long Island who were willing to help the family immigrate and adjust to their new life in the United States.

Family would always be family!

And though it may have been an unfortunate coincidence, shortly after Nonna Grazia had passed away, the family's *negozio* began losing business. Times were changing in their little Sicilian town; long-time customers moved away, supplier costs had increased, as did the worry lines in both Mamma and Papà's faces.

As a seven-year old though, Michelina was not privy to the anxieties of adulthood--that would come later. Instead she simply took each day as it arrived and wondered what they would all discover in America.

Exactly one week before they boarded their Boeing 767-300 aircraft for their flight to the New World, Michelina slipped away from her younger siblings and parents who were busy with a hundred details. She was one who could be alone without feeling lonely. This trait followed her into adulthood and as she would later observe, the experience would leave her feeling recharged.

Stepping outside into the brilliant heat of the Sicilian day, she crossed the semi-paved road and descended the stone steps adjacent to her Nonna's house. Pausing on the third step from the bottom, Michelina sprouted imaginary wings and leapt off the stairs tumbling playfully into the soft soil of her grandmother's garden. Directly in front of her was row after row of beautifully gnarled olive trees which never failed to provide the family with plenty of ripe olives. There were also grapes vines, fruit trees, wild flowers and her favorite of all, a huge fig tree planted by her Nonno or grandfather nearly forty years ago.

Michelina would often scurry up the tree, find a good seat and watch her tiny piece of the world go by. Of course, there were plenty of figs for the taking as well. For some time, she just rested, her back against the familiar bark, birds chirping and insects buzzing about, all telling their stories.

But then something changed. Something quite wonderful!

The air about her seemed to pulsate with a new vitality and Michelina began smelling the sweetest fragrance that she had ever remembered smelling. Oddly enough, she noticed that the birds had stopped singing and the insects were silenced. Though she did not feel frightened, her body began to tremble--one full step ahead of her understanding!

She then looked all around, first to her left side and then to the right.

She saw nothing. No one at all!

Instead an incredibly refreshing cool breeze swept in and around her. It was a wind that seemed alive and inviting. Michelina was captivated and it seemed as if something deep inside of her was very, very happy.

And then she saw Him…

He was the most beautiful man she had ever seen. Not handsome as some would consider it but altogether beautiful! He wore a robe that was whiter than lamb's wool and His face radiated love and kindness.

The Man's smile launched waves of joy within her but it was His eyes…which flashed and told amazing stories.

As she focused on His eyes, Michelina saw a reflection of herself. Her clothing and outward appearance was soiled and her face was masked with dirt and grime. Though she wanted to avoid the image she was tightly held in the grip of her own darkness. Instantly, Michelina began sobbing uncontrollably as the truth of her own nature struck her.

She was in such agony of soul that she literally fell out of the tree where she lay prostrate, shaking and sobbing with an uncontrollable sorrow.

The tears continue to flow until she felt a Hand gently lift her face to once again consider His eyes. This time though she was clean and clothed with the same brilliant whiteness that He wore. Without speaking an audible word, He whispered to her heart,

I love you Michelina and I will always love you child. You know who I am and I have chosen you to serve Me and love My people for when you love others you love Me as well.

I will open your eyes to see My kingdom and your ears to hear My words. This assignment will not always be an easy road but My grace will keep you.

My grace will always keep you in My love.

And then in a moment, Michelina found herself kneeling in the dirt on slightly banged up knees. *Ouch,* she thought to herself, *my knees hurt!* But then she felt a wave of incredible love followed by a joy which literally poured out of her.

Standing to her feet, Michelina lifted her hands to the heavens and cried out, *Thank You Jesus! Thank You for coming to me and cleansing me!*

For some time, the little girl who had just met the God of Creation stood in her Nonna's garden both weeping and laughing. She was truly alive for the first time in her young life and it was an amazing feeling.

But feelings would come and feelings would go.

Chapter 5

The mission was a go!

Without a spoken word, the eyes of the male agent announced the news to his female accomplice. Their masquerade as husband and wife had long achieved its purpose and those who knew them--or who thought they knew them, considered the relationship a model of marital bliss.

Their cover had been successfully built up over a ten-year period in which their import-export business became increasingly important to a country tottering on insolvency largely due to wave after wave of international sanctions. And while the nation's leader and his elites cared nothing for their poor and huddled masses, boys [and girls] must have their toys and the businessman and his *wife* were more than happy to supply the leadership with whatever pleasures they desired.

Requests for fine wine, clothing, jewelry, paintings, boats and even the latest techno-gadgets were all quickly delivered.

To the couple's great delight, the Supreme Leader possessed an insatiable appetite that outdistanced his underlings. He was a man who spared himself nothing even if he couldn't flaunt his wealth abroad. His list included palaces, a couple of yachts, billions in gold bullion and a fleet of highly sophisticated and heavily armored limousines. Dictators could never be too careful, even though they expend great resources in suppressing the masses.

Yet unknown to the corpulent ruler of one of the most repressive governments on the planet, each of his specially configured vehicles contained a miniaturized and undetectable GPS sensor buried deep in the floorboards. The sensors were part of a long-range contingency plan the protector state had for its often unruly and unpredictable vassal.

Its interests must always be preserved and especially when dealing with neighboring states and more importantly, the West. Call it insurance or whatever you prefer but friends were to be kept close and enemies even closer for who could know when either would turn on you?

Who could know?

The teachings of Sun Tzu were a gift of history. Enemies were to be engaged only when the time, terms, and terrain were advantageous for victory. This meant that in the end, weapons of time and patience would prove essential keys to victory.

Years, decades and even centuries were a form of foot soldiers that the United States and her allies were ill-equipped to employ. Yet these qualities had immense consequences for war, political aspirations, and economic developments--and of course, assassinations!

Chapter 6

Democratic People's Republic of Korea

W hat can be said about a 21st century country, isolated among all but a few nations on the planet, and forced into a virtual medieval state of existence? With nearly twenty-five million souls the Democratic People's Republic of Korea or DPRK was neither democratic nor in any sense of the word, a republic! Instead North Korea sported its own unique form of totalitarianism courtesy of two superpowers vying for strategic advantage in the post-World War II era.

After Korea's liberation from Japanese occupation in 1945, the territory above the 38th parallel had been occupied by the Soviets. Below the parallel, were the Americans! Caught in the middle of a Cold War between former allies were the Korean people. Each side retreated to their respective ideological camps and the South embraced democratic ideals and capitalism. The North...well the North Koreans, dove headfirst into a particularly oppressive and belligerent posture which was extreme by even Soviet and Communist Chinese standards.

Kim Gun Suk, the latest of the *Hermit Kingdom's* three post-war rulers became North Korea's supreme leader after the natural death of his father in 2011. Despite his relatively young age, he succeeded in carrying out his father's and grandfather's brutal policies; terrorizing both his people and those within reach of his formidable military.

His iron-fisted control however did have some drawbacks. In terms of reported dishonesty, North Korea tied with Somalia as the most corrupt country in the world. And while claiming 100 percent literacy, it's GDP per capital ranking of $1,800 was laughable when compared to its wealthier [and freer] brothers in the South who averaged $32,400. Military spending--always a marker for a nation's priorities and ambitions, was over twenty-two percent for the North and little more than two percent south of the demilitarized zone.

There were many other glaring distinctions between a once undivided people, mostly perpetuated by Kim Gun Suk's persistent paranoia and view of his own self-importance. That his people would suffer through pervasive food shortages, the threat of horrific labor camps, and the ever present secret subversions of informers and agents of the state, did not affect the so-called Great Leader in the least.

Beneath his chubby exterior was a heart completely devoid of compassion, mercy, or forgiveness. He learned to hate at an early age and the habit stuck.

It was that feature of his profile which kept observers guessing--never quite certain of Kim Gun Suk's true intentions. Over the years, his ranting and threats made for good headlines. He then raised the bar in March of 2016, warning that New York City *and all the people there would be killed immediately and the city would burn...to ashes!*

What was a reasonable person to think?

Moreover, what about Western intelligence agencies and especially that of the US national security community? Just more rhetoric from a poorly trained Shakespearian actor lacking the capacity to strike the US!

After all, in 2016, everyone knew the Hermit Kingdom did not have an ICBM capability.

Wasn't that right?

Chapter 7

Rockets, Missiles, and ICBMs

North Korean's rocket and missile program began in the early 1960s with production of multiple rocket launchers. In 1965, the Great Leader's grandfather decided to develop an indigenous ballistic missile capability. His justification was to deter or defeat U. S. military forces in addition to a growing apprehension regarding the defense commitments of his Soviet Union and Chinese allies.

Despite an uneasy alliance, the Soviets supplied the North Koreans with surface-to-ship missiles and FROG 5/7 rockets while the Chinese provided Surface Air Missiles [SAMs] and technical assistance. By the late seventies, Pyongyang had developed its infrastructure to the point where it began to reverse engineer Soviet made Scud B missiles. This led to a successful flight test of the Hwasong-5, a home-spun version of the Scud B.

In 1985, the North Koreans entered into a unique *buy- now-and-deliver-later* agreement with the Iranians who gladly bankrolled the Korean missile program for delivery of goods on a later date. Throughout the late eighties and nineties, Pyongyang rapidly advanced its technology to include development of an intermediate range Nodung missile. Flight tests were conducted in both Iran and Pakistan and the Nodung was fully deployed in 1995.

To further subsidize their efforts, the North Koreans adopted a page from their capitalistic enemies and began exporting Scuds and conventional weapons to any and all buyers. This served the dual purpose of improving their intermediate range missile program while also developing ICBMs capable of hitting the western regions of the United States.

Patiently, the Great Leader parried international outrage and various embargos in pursuit of the all-important long-range missile threat. In 2011, North Korea completed a ten-year construction project at its Sohae Satellite Launching Site. The new base had a moveable launch pad and all the necessary pieces to test an intercontinental missile. In response, many officials in previous administration began to develop migraine-like symptoms.

Reacting to sanctions, the regime agreed to a suspension of its long-range testing in February of 2012. However, the deal fell apart a short two months later when North Korean sent a satellite into orbit using a powerful Unha-3 rocket engine. Despite threats and political pressure, the Great Leader understood that his one ace in the hole rested on fielding a nuclear tipped ICBM. Once achieved, the North Koreans could take saber rattling to an entirely new level--backed by a credible existential threat at anyone threatening their sovereignty.

Throwing caution to the wind, the North Koreans continued their long-range tests further threatening the fragile peace on the Korean peninsula. In his annual New Year's speech in January of 2017, a cheerful Kim Gun Suk announced that the nation had finished plans to conduct its first ICBM test. Six week later, a first viewed solid fuels missile was launched harmlessly splashing down in the Sea of Japan some 500 kilometers away.

The North Koreans were close and soon there would be no stopping them from achieving their goal!

Later in July of 2017, they successfully flight-tested a Hwasong-14 missile with an estimated range of between 6,700 to 8.000 kilometers. Despite the U.S. president's famous Twitter comment that it *won't happen*--it did!

To the shock of many so-called experts, the Democratic People's Republic of Korea had crashed the gates of the ICBM club!

And it was anyone's guess what the cost of their membership would be!

Chapter 8

12 May 2017, Tehran, Islamic Republic of Iran

Putting down his headset, the Iranian Ministry of Intelligence officer swiveled in his chair and faced his superior. The highly secretive agency was created to replace SAVAK, the Shah's hated secret police, and though both organizations served much different ideologies, ironically their methods remained largely the same.

Standing up, the athletic man with closely cropped hair and a full beard, stretched, and then reported.

Our North Korean friends are like hornets flying in the face of the American president. Through years of weakness they allowed the Koreans to build nuclear weapons and now, they are wringing their hands because of an ICBM threat!

Replying, his commander asked,

We knew North Korea was racing to achieve an intercontinental launch capability. Our leaders are already in negotiations with Kim Gun Suk's regime to transfer that technology to our Islamic Republic.

With a humorless grin he added, *and, it will be largely paid for by the generous concessions made by President Rizzo's predecessor. That treaty made an utter fool of the Americans and their feckless allies.*

Let Allah be praised for that victory!

Putting on a serious look the commander continued,

Listen, I am not going to brief my superiors with information they already know. Tell me something substantive.

Turning to his desk the subordinate picked up a folder and handed it to the man who took several minutes to read the information.

Holding the folder in his hands, the senior intelligence officer seemed pleased.

Yes, this will do quite nicely. When did the North Koreans gain the capacity to miniaturize their warheads?

Quickly replying the analyst asserted, *our source in Pyongyang claims it was less than a month ago. That is something we must admire about the Koreans - their unrelenting tenacity. Though they are infidels they know how to achieve their goals in the face of global opposition.*

Sternly the senior officer responded.

I'm not concerned with Korean tenacity. I want to know if you are certain of their capabilities. And, do the Americans know?

The subordinate fielded both questions.

Yes, I am quite certain. As we speak, the Koreans are racing to miniaturize all sixty of their nuclear devices.

As for your second question, no--there is a great deal of speculation in the American media but no one representing their government has made statements regarding such a technological advancement.

The commanding officer, a survivor of many human wave attacks during the latter years of the Iran-Iraq War, was not known for showing emotions. But the information brought an uncommon smile to his face.

Good, very good! You have done well and I will remember this.

He then left the room for a briefing with Iran's religious and military leaders.

Chapter 9

15 May 2017, U.S. Capital Building

The Senate Armed Services Committee public hearing was crowded and all attention was on the four-star Air Force officer positioned behind the mike. The ranking Democrat on the Committee continued with his list of questions.

General, what do we know about the current North Korean ICBM threat?

Taking a sip of water, the second highest ranking officer in the U. S. military chain of command replied.

What the experts tell me is that the North Koreans have yet to demonstrate the capacity to do the guidance and control that would be required…

With obvious irritation, the Senator interrupted the general.

General with all due respect--this committee has been briefed on that information already. However, as every member of this committee will tell you it's the American people who want to know the real threat posed by the North Koreans and their missile program.

So, let me reframe my question. Are you saying that the North Koreans can now strike anywhere on U.S. soil...but without a measured degree of accuracy?

Holding his gaze on the senator, the career officer answered.

Yes, I am. North Korean ICBMs are capable of indiscriminately reaching the continental United States and certainly without precision.

With anger he did little to conceal, the senator continued.

Well that's just great general! A rogue nation can lob nukes on American soil but we shouldn't be too concerned because they are not very accurate!

Before yielding the floor to the chairman of the committee, the senator issued a final statement--and not just for the sake of the embattled general facing him.

All I can say is that this administration must do something about this threat and they better do it fast!

*****

Later that evening, the major news outlets camped on the uncertainty generated from the public hearing playing the *fear card* with a ruthless enthusiasm. Talking heads pounced on the four-star's unfortunate comments *that the North Koreans have yet to demonstrate the capacity to do the guidance and control that would be required...*

Serious-faced moderators looking directly into their monitors parroted a well-rehearsed mantra.

Apparently, the administration is quite unprepared to deal with the existential ICBM threat posed by North Korea's reckless government.

The narrative continued.

President Rizzo's bellicose comments and dismissive tweets regarding the North Korean leader and his nation must certainly be viewed as part of the problem. Such provocations are a slippery slope which the former administration had skillfully avoided.

All told, it was not a good night for the president and his team and it was certainly not a good night for the nation!

The Book of Psalms

Why do the nations rage and the people plot a vain thing? The kings of the earth set themselves, and the rulers take counsel together, against the LORD and against His Anointed, saying, let us break their bonds in pieces and cast away their cords from us.

He who sits in the heavens shall laugh; the Lord shall hold them in derision. Then He shall speak to them in His wrath, and distress them in His deep displeasure.

[Psalm 2:1-5]

Chapter 10

Summer 1982, East Garden City, New York

From high in the branches of a leafy Eastern Red Cedar a nine-year female voice descended below to her mother who had just stepped out to the backyard patio.

Mamma! Hello Mamma! Can I go over to Nonno's house? Can I please?

Glancing around and not seeing her daughter, Maria Tarrantino answered.

I want to see you and not just hear your voice. Come out from wherever you are and we'll talk about it.

In a flash Michelina slid down her favorite tree and ran over to her mother who asked,

Did you make your bed and clean up your room?

Flashing her famously hard-to-resist smile, the nine-year old replied,

Of course, Mamma! I took care of my room before I came downstairs for breakfast. I really want to see Nonno Tarrantino today and help him with his garden and chickens.

After a thoughtful pause, her mother conceded but then added a condition.

Okay Michelina, you can visit Nonno <u>but</u> you'll have to take your younger brother with you.

Knowing that her mother was unlikely to bend on taking her brother along, she halfheartedly answered.

Alright Momma, I'll take Roberto with me, and in a few minutes, she was out the front door with her younger brother tagging behind.

*****

It had been two years since the Tarrantino's landed in New York's JFK airport with all their earthly possessions carefully packed inside their hand-held luggage. Greeting them was Nonno Tarrantino, the family patriarch, and a large contingent of relatives and family friends who had made earlier transatlantic crossings.

In the manner of immigrants, the world over, Mario Tarrantino sought the support of kinsmen who knew the ropes and strange nuances of New World life. With his father's help, the son found a job and then purchased a modest house in East Garden City.

Hard working and thrifty, the Tarrantino's would eventually go into business for themselves as owners of a small restaurant, a departure from the *negozio* they had in Sicily, but one that showcased Maria's extraordinary culinary skills and Mario's business sense. Eventually, their family restaurant or *trattoria*, would become a local favorite featuring, Mamma's famous meatballs, pasta dishes, and desserts.

The genes passed on to Michelina who would one day take *Tarrantino's Trattoria* to a whole new level of gastronomic excellence. But that would be much later down life's often winding road.

Chapter 11

October 1986, Garden City, Long Island

Michelina sat nervously outside Mr. LaGiglia's office. Beside her was her best friend Mia and behind the Assistant Principal's closed door was Gloria, the third perpetrator of the crime of the century!

Mr. LaGiglia was a hulking and formidable sight especially for three young freshmen students. The former college football guard was six-foot four and it was a certainty that he would never see his former playing weight of three hundred pounds again! Yet it was not his intimidating physical presence that mattered most too each girl. Rather it was his dark, penetrating eyes that seemed to bore holes straight into your head. Even the most recalcitrant of high school misbehavers would eventually break under his *stare of doom*!

Alone in her thoughts, Michelina, who had adopted Mike as part of a new emerging identity, was resolutely beating herself up,

Why did I listen to them? I know better than this and I can just imagine what my parents are going to say?

Yet the alleged *criminal act* was just another in a long list of lively pranks that the administrators of Garden City High School would endure throughout the years.

In planning their caper, the three *perps* had intended to simply hide the school's mascot before the big homecoming game rally. Their intended target was none other than Mr. LaGiglia who was the official mascot handler--a role he cherished and fought to preserve although there were few competitors for the honor. Not everyone was interested in handling an adult *Falco peregrinus anatum,* more commonly known as the American peregrine falcon!

The school's raptor was a beautiful bird about the size of a large crow with a blue-grey back and a white undercarriage. It was the fastest creature in all the animal kingdom with a clocked speed of 242 miles an hour. Yet there was one other fact Mike and her friends had overlooked in their secret conspiracy--the peregrine was also called a *duck hawk!*

And you guessed it--Garden City had its fair share of ponds, small lakes and of course, ducks!

On the day of the rally, Mike served as a reluctant scout while Mia and Gloria went inside the annex where the falcon spent most of its time in its large cage or *mew.* The girls knew that Mr. LaGiglia would have the bird in its special carrying cage and ready to transport to the football stadium. Quickly grabbing the carrier, the two girls raced to a side door hoping to stash the falcon behind the building. Wide eyed, Mike watched her giggling friends rush by with an equally wide-eyed peregrine falcon loudly shrieking its displeasure.

And then Mia tripped...

Mia's right leg then caught Gloria's left foot resulting in a Houston control launch of the falcon cage. Landing unceremoniously on its side, the door of the cage popped open and in a flash, the bird was in the air fiercely expressing its pleasure as it soared higher and higher into the bright open skies.

That's when Mike knew they would receive the death penalty!

*****

Suddenly the door opened and Mr. LaGiglia pointed to Mia. A shaken Gloria made her way to a chair and quietly sat down without making eye contact with her friend.

Mike found little solace in her thoughts. She had acted out of character yielding to peer-pressure, one of the oldest of all temptations.

Why God? Why did I agree when everything inside of me was saying no way? Even though we intended to return the falcon as soon as it was safe to do so, I had no business causing Mr. LaGiglia and others trouble.

God, I have no defense as I know right from wrong. Please forgive me!

And right there in the assistant principal's office at Garden City High, God Almighty had a meeting with his daughter. He willingly forgave, corrected, and then renewed a right spirit

51

within her. He reminded her that those who God calls have a responsibility to do what is right and walk in truth. This would be especially true for Mike as she entered deeper into her prophetic calling as one who sees and hears for God.

*****

Suddenly she became aware of a large looming presence looking down at her. Glancing around she saw Mia and Gloria next to one another and then lifting her gaze she saw the eyes!

Come in Mike. I've saved you for last! Do you know how many ducks a peregrine falcon can eat when it's very hungry?

And then Mr. LaGiglia closed the door.

Chapter 12

September 1986, Garden City, Long Island

Three weeks into her junior year, Mike trudged along until she got to her last class of the day featuring a full forty-five minutes with the notorious Ms. Bush. Her teacher was as old as Methuselah and she reportedly studied under Hipparchus in a little hut somewhere in the Greek islands! Her pedagogical style borrowed a page from Karl Marx's Communist Manifesto and most students simply resigned themselves to a year spent in a mathematical gulag.

She took her seat next to Mia with Gloria quietly chatting away behind her. Together, the three female amigos believed they could endure anything--even Ms. Bush!

Without warning the no-nonsense teacher marched into the room and took a customary position behind her desk. With a baleful look that dared anyone to challenge her, she started barking orders.

Attention class!

Quietly--and I mean quietly, take out your trig book, notepad, and a few pencils. If you need to sharpen a pencil do it now and not during the lesson. I have a lot of material to cover today and I want you to empty your heads of everything but trigonometry right now!

Next, take out last night's homework and we'll quickly review your answers and then…

And then the door opened and the most gorgeous male that any female student ever laid eyes on walked into the classroom. Amazingly, the face that broke a thousand hearts also had a voice.

Hi! I'm Mackenzie O'Brien but I prefer to be called Mac. My family and I just moved into town from Annapolis, Maryland last week.

Then with a disarming smile he added, *I have my class registration slip right here.*

Startled by the unexpected interruption and the handsome young man standing in front of her, Ms. Bush seemed at a loss for words. Meanwhile, Gloria was furiously poking Mike in her back while loudly whispering,

Look at that guy--he's unbelievably cute! I think I'm having a mini heart attack--please revive me Mike!

Annoyed and smarting from the jab in her back, Mike quickly turned in her seat and was just about to give her friend a piece of her mind when she heard a frosty voice!

Ms. Tarrantino!

What do you think you are doing? Who gave you permission to turn around in your seat and disrupt my room? Young lady I'll see you right after class.

Publicly humiliated and with a red blush spreading across her olive-skinned face, Mike turned around only to discover both Ms. Bush <u>and the new boy</u> staring directly at her.

She thought to herself,

This can't be happening to me. The cutest boy on the planet must be thinking I'm an idiot? I'm going to make Gloria pay for this!

But her angst quickly dissipated when she realized that Mackenzie *Mac* O'Brien was staring at her with a look which sparked the woman inside for the first time. For a moment everything and everyone in the room faded as their eyes met-- of course, with proper introductions to follow.

Mike's heart started pounding and with great difficulty she forced her eyes to focus on the homework sitting on her desk. Meanwhile she felt a rising joy that was difficult to contain--yet somehow hindered by Ms. Bush's presence.

Mike was almost seventeen years old and like every young female around the globe she had thoughts about *him*--that right guy who would suddenly appear on the horizon and sweep her off her feet into unending marital bliss.

She realized her expectation was an idyllic notion unsupported by the death spiral of traditional marriages in the United States. Yet for years she had been praying for a marriage arranged in heaven but lived out in faith and love on earth.

She wanted God's best and she told Him over and over that she was willing to wait for that right man.

And now her Prince Charming had arrived, risking a painful death or worse, in taking every opportunity to look over at her when Ms. Bush's back had been turned to the class. There he was--heaven's answer right there in Ms. Bush's seventh period trig class!

Not a single word had yet been spoken between them but it didn't matter. Mike's *knowing* gift had switched into high gear.

He's the one God isn't he! Yes, yes, yes--I will soon meet the man I will one day marry!

Chapter 13

Garden City, New York

Mac had a lot to think about on the way home after his first day at Garden City High. First, he had met after trig class the most incredibly beautiful girl he ever laid eyes on. Next, he was excited to have met Mr. Clancy Dermot, the legendary coach of the school's championship lacrosse team. Mac had started playing the game in Maryland and he was one hundred percent hooked! The oldest team sport in America, lacrosse required speed, strength, agility and most importantly, a mental toughness that Mac found exhilarating.

Physically, Mac was an impressive young man standing a hair over six feet and supported by one-hundred and eighty pounds of exceptional athleticism. He was the perfect midfielder with the speed of an attacker and the strength required of a defensive player. He was also a smart player who inevitably helped his teammates to play better.

But as much as Mac loved lacrosse it came in a close second to his dream of becoming a naval aviator. His mom and dad supported him in this goal and when necessary, they applied a strict form of parental love in keeping his train on the right tracks. They asked for his best and he responded--in the classroom, on the playing field, and doing what was necessary to earn an appointment to the Naval Academy at Annapolis. Growing up in a military family, the U.S. Navy had an undeniable influence on Mac's life with a history dating back to his paternal grandfather.

*****

The year was 1941 and James O'Brien had married Helen Baker right out of high school. A year later the couple celebrated the birth of their first son James Jr. The following year Helen became pregnant again but the war in the Pacific interrupted their family plans.

Like so many other Americans, the elder James had been enraged by the attack on Pearl Harbor. Tough as it was, he left Helen, little James, and the son he would never see to enlist in the Navy in February of 1943. Eventually he was assigned to the ill-fated USS *St. Lo,* a Casablanca-class escort carrier that saw action during the Battle of Leyte Gulf.

Regrettably, the *St. Lo* became the first major warship to have been sunk by a Japanese kamikaze attack during the war in the Pacific.

On that fateful 25th of October 1944, James was engaged in refueling activities when a Japanese Zero crashed into the flight deck and penetrated to the port side of the hangar deck below. The *St. Lo* was soon engulfed in a huge fireball followed by six secondary explosions. Mortally wounded, she sank within thirty minutes of the attack taking the lives of 113 men.

James O'Brien was among those whose remains would never be found!

On a quiet sunny November day, Helen was sitting on the steps of their rented house with James Jr. at her side and his brother Jack on her lap. She was tired from a fitful night in which she fought and lost a battle for sleep.

She was about to lose much more.

Slowly pulling up to the curb was a specially marked Western Union car with a grim-faced messenger at the wheel. At that time, the U.S. War Department used telegraphs to notify families that their soldier, sailor or airman had been wounded, missing in action, or killed in combat.

Instantly Helen knew her husband would not be coming home and the tears began flowing before the man even stepped out of his car.

*****

Eighteen years after the sinking of the *St. Lo,* Jack enlisted in the Navy. Law enforcement appealed to him and he became a Master of Arms serving time on board ships as well as shore duty. The Master of Arms rating was one of the oldest in the military dating back to the inception of the U.S. Navy.

Jack was good at what he did and promotion followed promotion. After twelve years as an enlisted man, he became a warrant officer. Later in his career he successfully applied for duty with the Naval Investigative Service or NIS. Beginning in

1983, the NIS established a terrorist watch center after the tragic bombing of the Marine Corps barracks in Beirut, Lebanon. Two years later, the NIS was renamed the Naval Security and Investigative Service [NCIS] and elevated to a full command with its own two-star commander billet.

Nearing the end of an eventual thirty-year career, Jack began looking for a close-out assignment that would bring a sense of permanence to a wife and two sons who had moved ten times in the previous twenty-six years. Pulling in a few favors, he managed to get reassigned from his former duty station at Annapolis, Maryland to a relatively new NCIS office in the New York City metropolitan area.

His wife Gwen had family living in and around Garden City centrally located in Long Island's Nassau County. It would be an easy commute to his office, flush with relatives, and perhaps more importantly, Garden City had one of the best high school lacrosse programs in the state.

*****

Jack retired from the Navy in January of 1993 and using his own terms, he simply *shifted gears* while working for himself as a private investigator until 9/11. After Tom Ridge stood up the newly formed Department of Homeland Security or DHS in 2002, Jack decided to take a stand with the former Pennsylvania governor and at the tender age of 59 he became a member of Homeland Security team.

For a man like Jack O'Brien, retirement wasn't an option when his country remained in danger.

Chapter 14

26 May 2017, Pyongyang

I t was just another overcast day in a nation known for its darkness. The Hermit Kingdom, a term referring to Korea's former two-hundred-year period of isolation while under Chinese control, had willfully walled itself in again in the 21st century. Although several other nations vied for its unenviable status, North Korea remained one of the most repressive and brutal regimes on the planet.

Reported across news outlets, the country was run by an enigmatic *off-the-track* millennial with a penchant for brinksmanship. As a third generational despot, he ascended to power after the death of his father who died suddenly from a massive heart attack. His succession had been made possible through the efforts of his mother--a favorite among his father's many mistresses. Along with other siblings, the heir apparent was groomed at the finest international boarding schools where he began his study of the Western mind and culture. Returning home his education continued as he observed his father wield absolute control over a regime in which no one was to be trusted--not even family, relatives or the most earnest of adoring citizens. Over and over, his father would tell him:

Never trust a single soul around you. Keep your eyes on everyone and recognize that betrayal comes from the closest hand!

In the harsh world of his own creation, these words would be a key to his survival.

*****

With motors running and under the watchful eyes of a small army of heavily armed guards, the motorcade awaited the arrival of their *Peerless Leader*. This was to be a short transit from the ruler's palace to a special hardened bunker buried one hundred feet underground on the northern perimeter of the capital city of Pyongyang. The route was always varied and armored limousines and military escort vehicles would often separate into two or three columns as they speed across largely empty boulevards. Security details and drivers were frequently rotated and only but a handful of people were involved in planning the Leader's movements.

The issue today was in response to the ramped-up rhetoric and increasingly severe economic pressures created by the United States and her newly elected president. Despite a small physique and the plain round facial features of his grandfather, Kim Gun Suk possessed the fierce determination and iron will of a junkyard dog. He would not be cowered and in the upcoming meeting a response would be carefully laid out and plotted among the military and political attendees.

Suddenly the Leader and his entourage emerged and his double rapidly entered the first of two limousines sandwiched between two 6 x 6 armored personnel carriers or APCs, each equipped with two heavy 14.5 mm machine guns. Inside each APC sat six Special Forces troops along with three crew members. At the last moment, the real leader of the Democratic People's Republic of Korea turned abruptly from entering the 2nd limousine and he enters a third and trailing APC in the motorcade.

With the roar of revved up engines, the vehicles exit the palace gate quickly accessing the nearby thoroughfare. Overhead a military helicopter provides cover.

The shell game had begun.

*****

Moments later, two hand-held and completely sanitized micro drones are launched from the fifth story roof of a business office several kilometers from the convoy's destination. One is a decoy and the other, a kamikaze drone, loaded with enough high explosive materials to destroy completely it's intended target.

Nearing the bunker, the convoy must briefly exit the motorway and pass through a few connecting city streets before their final arrival. Precisely at this leg of their route, the decoy drone draws the attention of the accompanying military helicopter. As the pilot seeks to lock on it with his fire control radar, the second drone makes its unnoticed descent. Suddenly the quiet of the city is disrupted by a blinding flash and a tremendous explosion.

Like a dying animal, the second limousine lies on its side, its top completely ripped off revealing the mangled remains of those unfortunate enough to have been inside. Pieces of the vehicle litter the road many of which are still smoldering from the blast.

The scene is chaotic! Yet today the dead would have to fend for themselves as the remaining vehicles speed around the wreckage intent on delivering their precious cargo to the intended bunker.

Arriving at their destination, North Korea's heroic leader steps out of his APC in a rage! With his face contorted in fury he launched into a tirade which left those around him trembling for their lives.

Who did this! Who tried to kill me? How did anyone know I had planned on using the second limousine? Can anyone tell me how that was possible?

I've been betrayed.

Then looking at the bewildered on-site commander, Kim Gun Suk screamed,

Arrest every man in my motorcade and use every means to find out who betrayed me! Do it now!

Still shaking with anger, the Great Leader stalked off leaving in his wake the hopeless looks of a disposable security team.

Chapter 15

With the president on a six-day Asian junket to ratchet down tensions on the Korean Peninsula, Sam Blackstone had his hand on the helm of the White House ship until his boss got back.

And it was some-kind-of-a-week!

Prior to taking a seat in another urgent Situation Room meeting, he tried to picture what retiring in a warm place like Florida or Southern California would look like. No stress and plenty of time to go to the beach, play a few rounds of golf, and totally indulge the grandchildren. However, the pleasant images quickly faded as the lights dimmed for a live streaming of an unfolding terrorist attack in London.

At first glance, the Vice President caught himself thinking, *oh no, not again* as the camera panned a frantic mob of people fleeing from the carnage taking place during the FA Cup Finals at Wembley Stadium, the city's largest football arena.

With nearly 500,000 CCTV cameras in the Greater London area, virtually every area of the city was under some sort of watchful eye, yet surveillance alone did not deter suicide bombers from attacking their targets. In the London attack, a suicide bomber detonated a sanitation truck loaded with explosives fifty yards from the Bobby Moore entrance of the stadium. As expected, crowds surged out of the stadium's remaining west and east entrances where they were ambushed by masked men brandishing Kalashnikov assault rifles.

As the VP watched in real time, London's tactical units were engaged in a fierce fire fight with a handful of terrorists who had withdrawn in good military order from the parking lot to take cover in the stadium. Meanwhile scores of bodies lay still on the ground and despite the on-going battle, emergency personnel were placing themselves in harm's way to retrieve the dead and wounded.

It was a nightmarish scene and one Sam Blackstone would soon not forget. Casualty figures in the hundreds would later shock the nation and the world community.

*****

ISIS later claimed responsibility for the attack with pledges to continue punishing the Brits for their war crimes in Iraq and Syria. Threats were also made to the United States through a video clip of a balaclava covered spokesman shouting into a camera.

America, do not think the Atlantic Ocean will protect you from our fury! Your soldiers, aircraft, tanks, and drones have killed countless Muslim men, women and children. And now your time to fear and die in pain has come.

We are already among you and we have a very big surprise for you!

Yes, a very big surprise!

Shaking his head at this latest threat, the Vice President turned to his personal aid and said,

Get in contact with Bill Brighton and have him schedule a meeting of the NSA first thing tomorrow morning. I want to know how we're planning on stopping these savages from committing a similar Wembley event in this country.

The aid replied,

I'll get on it right away Mr. Vice President!

Chapter 16

I t was the President's first day back from his exhausting Pacific trip and thankfully, the Oval Office was unusually quiet and devoid of people. The 45th president of the United States enjoyed the silence as he sat behind the *Resolute* desk, one of only six desks to grace the room and one preferred by the six previous residents. The wood had been carved from the HMS Resolute--a gift from Queen Victoria to Rutherford B. Hayes, the 19th president of an emerging power in the world.

It was said that Jacqueline Kennedy had found the desk languishing in the White House broadcast room and after having it restored she brought it back into the Oval Office.

It was another notch in Jackie's illustrious saddle!

President Matthew Rizzo's amazing climb to the top of America's political ladder had been both stunning and polarizing. His candidacy, campaign, and nomination defied the odds makers, political pundits, and just about every polling firm in the nation. He was a dark horse candidate and disparaged for having been born with a silver spoon in his hand.

But he had taken what good fortune had offered and through *street smarts* and an admirable work ethic he discovered how to create wealth and opportunity for himself and others as well. Yet, his blunt mannerisms and success enraged many on both sides of the political spectrum. He was an outsized outsider who jolted the sensitivities of those who lived within the capital's beltline and who preferred a *business as normal* administration.

They would never get that from Matthew Rizzo!

Right then, a sharp quick knock preceded the door being flung open by the President's petite and fiery special counselor, Katie Hatcher.

More rumblings from the news outlets Mr. President! Honestly, it never seems to stop and I'm getting tired with it.

Katie was a fierce loyalist and defender of the president's policies as well as his character. Because of her loyalties, she often found herself in the crosshairs of an increasingly hostile media waging an undeclared war of words, innuendos, and outright accusations. The attacks, starting before the inauguration, sadly introduced a new era of hostile reporting unlike any in the history of the office.

What's going on now, asked the people's choice-or at least the choice of nearly 63 million Americans.

Oh, much of the same--only further echoed by every Democratic leader in both houses and a slew of clueless Hollywood stars and starlets!

It's pathetic Mr. President. No one seems to care that we're making progress on your promises to the American people. It's as if the nation's welfare has taken a back seat to ideologues and loud mouths that could care less about what really matters to the people of this country.

Reaching across his desk, he gently patted her hand saying, *I understand Katie but I think we all realized it would be tough going-- though maybe not this tough! Anyway, we must not lose our focus although I'll admit the New Yorker in me would like to punch out a few editors and columnists.*

Then leaning back in his chair, he flashed his signature smile and said, *and that would be a real story!*

Katie replied, *Please Mr. President, don't even think about it* and they both shared a good laugh, always a welcomed tonic for the stresses of the office.

They were still chuckling when another knock on the door announced the arrival of Vice President Sam Blackstone.

Good morning Mr. President and welcome back. Glancing over at the special counselor's familiar face, he added,

Hello Katie and I are happy to see that something has cheered the both of you!

The President replied,

Hi Sam, good to see you! Katie was just trying to convince me from getting in the ring with a few so-called journalists.

Katie flashed a smile and added,

That's right Mr. President. I don't think any of us could live with those headlines!

At that, Sam Blackstone's voice and facial features took on a more serious tone.

Mr. President, I know we have a scheduled meeting later this afternoon but I felt it important to personally bring you up to speed on the situation in London.

With an alarmed look, the President asked,

Don't tell me there's been another attack?

No sir, but British MI5 has credible evidence that ISIS has flipped the go-active switch on their cells throughout the UK. I took a brief call from the Prime Minister who was understandably quite concerned.

I recommend we schedule an NSA meeting and get the latest information from our intelligence sources.

The President sat down shaking his head.

Go ahead Sam. Pull the meeting together and make sure it gets on my calendar. Sometimes I don't know what's worse, dealing with the media, terrorist attacks in Europe, or that crazy little man in North Korea.

But of course, history will help make that distinction!

Chapter 17

June 1988, Garden City, New York

The graduation was a class act--a well-orchestrated pageantry that met the expectations of Garden City High's largely upper middle class parents. The school's nationally recognized athletic programs and college-preparatory curriculum was precisely what interested many families to move into the area.

As the program unfolded, Mike stood with Mac in their gowns in a long winding line filled with other expectant graduates. Shortly each one would mount the stage featuring the school's colors, proudly walk in front of a large crowd of well-wishers, and receive their coveted diplomas. For Mac, graduation was merely a launching pad to his appointment at the U.S. Naval Academy at Annapolis. His hard work on the field and in the classroom paid expected dividends. In August he would become a midshipman, continue to play lacrosse, and ultimately, become a naval aviator. His dreams were unfolding before his eyes which included a shiny red 1964 ½ Ford Mustang convertible with a four-barrel 289 engine as a graduation gift from his parents. Mike on the other hand was given a high mileage 1967 VW bug with a large dent in the rear fender on the passenger's side of the car.

Sometimes life did not seem fair at all!

But Mike had different ambitions. She wanted her own business and the ability to be her own boss. Her plan would be a perfect fit to her strong, determined, and independent spirit-- a truth Mac discovered early in their budding romance. Although Mike was not much of an athlete, she was exceptionally bright which led to her acceptance at Cornell University, located in upstate New York. The school offered Mike a generous scholarship package supplemented by a substantial grant from the Italian-American Society. Her parents managed the rest of her tuition for her undergraduate studies.

Although their paths seemed to go in opposite directions, the young couple was certain they were meant to be together. Wisely, they also knew each one had a lot of growing up to do. Consequently, when it was time to go off to their respective schools, they prayerfully handed their relationship over to God while promising to stay in touch often.

While away from each other and their families, they would deal with academic rigors, but more importantly their adult personalities would be forged and their goals in life redefined. Behind the scenes, the Spirit of God had an entirely different set of spiritual objectives waiting for each one of them.

Ultimately, God would use their time apart much like a pre-marriage class that took years instead of days to complete.

As Mac and Mike would discover, the One who held eternity in His hands, seemed to ignore watches, calendars, and other conventional measures of time. Instead, He ran Planet Earth and the lives of His children from a heavenly perspective that at times could be downright exasperating but in the end always perfect on arrival.

Chapter 18

Summer 1992, Long Island, New York

F ounded in 1845, the Naval Academy sat on 338 manicured acres in Annapolis, Maryland where the Severn River empties into Chesapeake Bay. As a midshipman, Mac majored in Political Science and Government with a minor in International Studies. For Mac, his studies were a means to an end and that end had wings and at least one jet engine! Consequently, he was overjoyed with his selection to Primary Flight Training at Naval Air Station Whiting Field, located in Florida's Panhandle.

Meanwhile after four years at Cornell's prestigious business school, Mike was flooded with attractive offers to work for some of the large financial houses in New York City. Although flattered by the interest, her separation from Mac had developed into an acute yearning to become Mrs. O'Brien. Despite the encouragement of her professors to go on for an

MBA, she was quite happy to lay it aside to become a wife and hopefully, a mother.

The following week both would be back on Long Island and staying with their parents. It would be an excellent time for the prince to ask his lady-in-waiting to come live with him in the palace!

But things didn't go the way either one of them had hoped!

*****

After a great day at Jones Beach, the couple had been loading up Mac's convertible Mustang before the perfect storm struck!

Mac, I need to talk to you about something that is really bothering me.

We've been together all week and all I've heard you talk about has been Flight Training, Flight Training, and then what kind of fighter you hope to get. And then in one great, less self-absorbed moment, you managed to bring up our future together!

Is this what I should expect--to be little more than your wingman in life?

In the tradition of most men throughout the ages, Mac was dumbfounded. Mike was clearly angry--maybe seething was a better description. She sat in the passenger seat staring straight ahead and then,

Take me home Mac. Right now!

Trying to regain some hope for arbitration, Mac turned and faced his stoic passenger. *Mike, what's wrong? Why are you so upset with me? Didn't we have a wonderful time today?*

The silence was deafening.

Please Mike, you know that I love you. I have always loved you ever since the first day I saw you in Ms. Bush's' class. You were beautiful then and now you're still the most beautiful girl in the world to me.

Again, the gates to the city remained double-barred and impenetrable.

They continued sitting silently in the parking lot until an attendant told Mac that they would need to leave. Halfway back to Garden City Mike finally spoke…and this time fast flowing tears had replaced the anger.

Mac, when I first saw you in Ms. Bush's class my heart did a double flip. I had plenty of suitors but none of them interested me. Long ago, I prayed that God would give me a man who would really love me. I also asked that when I met that man I would know that he was the one.

They rode on in silence for several miles and then Mike quietly asked,

Mac, is the Navy and a flying career more important to you than me?

In response, Mac slowed the car and pulled the Ford off to a grassy area along the Meadowbrook State Parkway. Turning to face his wounded princess hot tears began welling up in his eyes.

Mike, I am so very sorry. I realize now how I continued to share my flying plans at your expense. I never intended to do that. I guess I just got caught up with it all.

Will you please forgive me? I was insensitive and as you pointed out, self-absorbed. I messed up a lovely day and it was entirely my fault.

It didn't take long for the hurt feelings to leave and once Mike let go of her hurt, she found it quite easy to forgive Mac.

Oh Mac, of course I forgive you. It's just that I felt like our lives together had taken a second seat to the Navy.

Mike then leaned over, gave Mac a gentle kiss on his cheek, and whispered, *Mac, I love you so.*

With an ear-to-ear smile, Mac then leaned over and stuck his hand in the glove compartment. Feeling around until he found what he wanted, he then pulled out a small but beautifully wrapped box.

He handed it to Mike and said, *please open it up.*

Nervously Mike tore the wrapping and lifted the lid of the box. Staring up at her was a gorgeous one carat diamond engagement ring.

Then sitting in a 1964 ½ Ford Mustang convertible on the side of Meadowbrook State Parkway, Mike heard the words she had so longed for.

Mike, will you marry me and love me forever?

*****

Of course, Mike said yes and the wedding took place in a lovely little chapel on the north shore of Long Island. Afterwards, Mike's family pulled out the stops with a superb reception at a fancy reception hall further out on the island. A few days later, their church gave the couple a second less formal wedding reception.

After the festivities, the couple escaped family, friends, and Long Island for a long anticipated get-away. Flying from JFK International Airport to Miami Beach, they boarded a cruise ship for a glorious six-day floating honeymoon in the Caribbean.

Once they got back, *Mike* would begin a crash course on becoming the wife of a naval aviator!

Chapter 19

6 June 2017, Pyongyang, North Korea

The man's ranting was not only heard but felt like a stabbing pain in the core of their being! For what seemed like an eternity, the men in the Great Leader's inner circle endured a continuous stream of accusations and threats:

How dare they? Do they know who they are dealing with? Do they think I am without resources? That I cannot respond?

Try to assassinate me--in my own capital city! How could this happen? How could the Americans know the time and precise destination of my route? I will repay them...

Continuing until utterly spent, the dictator fell back heavily into his chair. The room was deathly quiet as every eye remained riveted on the man who held their lives in his clenched hands.

Deep breaths broke the uneasy silence as the leader continued to fix his steely gaze at the back wall of the underground conference room. Finally, the round little man who terrorized a nation stood to his feet.

A fearful trembling began to crawl up the legs of those in attendance. They had seen this drama unfold--in fact many times before as real and imagined threats and offenses were tried in a court of One. There was death in those decisions, even the most gruesome of executions that only an unhinged person could conceive. Military leaders, government elites, and even members of his own family were all tried and convicted without the slightest hope of mercy.

It was clear that the nation's despotic ruler was fed by the same evil DNA material of his father and grandfather.

Or were Kim Gun Suk's genes even worse?

Then remarkably, while still focused on the man who held their destinies in his hand, an unexpected transformation took place. Gone were the screams and ranting. Absent was the icy gaze and angry countenance. Instead a faint smile now framed a face that almost appeared angelic. His voice was low and controlled and each word was chosen carefully.

We will repay the Americans in a way they will never forget. As they sought to take my life, now many will suffer the consequences.

Their president has tried to bully me and strangle the lifeblood of our glorious country. His forces have surrounded us and he continues to plot against us with those South Korean dogs. He sent his lackeys to my capital city to do me harm. And now...

Yes now, I will strike back at the city where he made his billions.

Momentarily collecting his thought, the Great Leader almost glowed as he continued,

Yes, I will indeed strike New York City--the very apple of his eye!

The shocked looks on the faces of the attendees were quickly stifled knowing that to disagree was a death sentence. Then a smattering of handclaps grew into a crescendo as each person silently pondered the next move of their leader.

They did not have long to wait!

Thank you, comrades. Yes indeed, thank you for your hearty endorsement of my brilliant plan. I can see how enthused you are and how grateful you are that I was spared the assassin's plot.

You are trusted advisors and members of my inner circle and you have no doubt given much thought to this latest plot against my life. This must be true especially as the people in this room alone knew my plans that day.

With a hearty laugh, Kim Gun Suk added, *and comrades, I did not tell the Americans!*

Still chuckling over his comment, he continued, *but someone here did and this knowledge pains me so. This pain must be absolved. And it shall.*

Then turning to General Park, his most senior military officer, the Great Leader said,

You my good general will be the first to undergo a most thorough examination of truth. Pausing to let the words sink in, he added, *and fear not for you will be joined by all the other truth-seekers in this room!*

With great satisfaction, North Korea's leader noted the terror-filled looks now staring back at him. Flashing a broad smile completely devoid of human warmth, he continued.

I am convinced that each of you will find truth and that truth will indeed set you free!

Then abruptly a command was given.

Guards!

Escort General Park out of the room! The rest of you please remain in your seats.

We must not rush the progress of truth.

At that, the man without a conscience, walked out of the room deep in thought. The attack had to be momentous and untraceable. It had to wound a great nation in a way it had never been wounded before.

Standing in a broad hallway lined with heavily armed soldiers, he had one more thought.

What a chore! I'll now have to find a new group of underlings!

Chapter 20

12 June 2017, White House, Washington DC

The National Security Act of 1947 led to sweeping changes in the way the United States developed and implemented its foreign policies. The Act led to the creation of a National Security Council [NSC] placed under the Executive Office of then president Harry S. Truman. The NSC was designed to promote coordination among the Army, Marine Corps, Air Force, Navy and other instruments of foreign policy to include the Central Intelligence Agency, which was also created under Truman's signature piece of legislation.

The bottom line was that the State Department could no longer independently develop and coordinate U.S. foreign policy in the face of a hostile and growing Soviet communism threat.

Shortly after taking office, President Rizzo moved some chess pieces and required the attendance of the Joint Chiefs of Staff and the Directors of the CIA and National Intelligence to the Principal's Committee, a cabinet-level senior forum chaired by the current appointed National Security Advisor, Bill Brighton.

Today's meeting would include the Principal's Committee along with the President, Vice President, the DHS Secretary, and the Ambassador to the United Nations. Two uniforms from the Defense Intelligence Agency and a CIA suit stood off to the side of the briefing podium.

With all attendees present the President nodded his head to start. First stepping up was a slightly graying but ramrod straight Air Force Lieutenant Colonel.

Good morning Mr. President and attendees. I'm Lieutenant Colonel Bill Northrup and I'll get right to the point sir. Four days ago, the chatter we usually receive from our monitoring installations on the peninsula spiked. The spike continued for three days and then dropped off the table.

The President questioned, *how unusual is this type of thing Colonel?*

Well sir, I've been involved with monitoring North Korean activities at least five years and I've never seen anything like it. They are quite savvy and they know we have every electronic ear in our inventory listening in.

Okay what's your take Colonel?

The Director of the Defense Intelligence Agency slightly nodded and Northrup answered,

Sir, something big must have taken place in the regime. Something out of the ordinary!

Replacing Lieutenant Colonel Northrup at the podium was a serious looking Navy captain.

Mr. President I'm Captain Mike Irons and our naval intelligence gathering assets can confirm what Bill Northrup just shared with you. I'm sure you are aware sir that we have subs sitting offshore the peninsula and pulling in signals 24/7.

We saw the same spike and the same drop off.

With keen interest, America's chief executive spoke up.

Thank you Captain and do you share your colleague's view that something out of the ordinary has taken place in the regime?

Before yielding the podium, Captain Irons replied,

Yes sir, I do.

Clearing his throat, the Director of the CIA then introduced the last presenter of the day.

Mr. President this is Sal Delgardo, one of our top analysts. Smiling, the Director added, *this is his first trip here sir and hopefully he'll want to come back again!*

Turning to Delgardo the President quipped,

Listen Sal, your secrets will be safe with us!

Smiling, Sal Delgardo proceeded;

Yes Mr. President I'm happy to know the information I share with you today will remain safe!

As you know Sir, the North Korean missile program has been on a fast track to develop an ICBM capability. With each failed test, they have managed to learn from their mistakes, a path that has been taking them ever closer to their long-range delivery goals.

At any rate, we've spent a considerable amount of time and resources trying to project a date when they will reach an initial operating capacity in their long-range missile program. Our analysis drawn from current CIA's resources, coupled with the information just shared by the previous presenters, suggests that they are almost there!

I cannot give you a precise date sir but the CIA's position is that North Korea's next launch could demonstrate an ICBM capability.

A deep silence swept around the room as the implication of a rogue state with an arsenal of nuclear tipped ICBMs sank in. Then, looking around the table where some of the nation's best and brightest minds sat, the president said,

Ladies and gentlemen, I think we all need to come up with a workable solution very soon--and I mean very soon!

Now, if there's nothing else on the agenda I think I've had all the good news I can stand today!

Good day!

Chapter 21

According to his instructions, at precisely 7:00 A.M the president's personal secretary knocked twice on the door to the Oval Office, entered with a steaming cup of freshly brewed black coffee, and then rehearsed his schedule for the day.

With a steady cheerful bearing that served her well during the last two administrations, Maddie Western connected with her new boss. *Good morning Mr. President and how are you feeling today?*

I'm doing well Maddie. The nation and world however remain a mess!

Setting his coffee on his desk Maddie replied,

Yes sir, Mr. President but that's why the American people elected you to office. You're the 45th president to grab the baton and get the job done.

Thanks Maddie. You're a bright light to my sometimes-overcast mornings. Laughing aloud the president quipped. *Remind me to put you in for a raise!*

I will indeed Mr. President. I will indeed!

Opening a beautifully bound leather folder, Maddie pulled out the president's agenda and began.

Now for your schedule today, you'll meet with the White House Chief of Staff at 8:00 am for forty-five minutes followed by a 10:00 o'clock session with the National Security Council. And by the way, the Vice President will also be there having returned from his trip to Europe.

Very good Maddie! Can you get me some time with him today? We need to catch up on his visit.

Not missing a beat, Maddie replied, *I've already taken care of that sir. You'll meet with the Vice President right after the NSA meeting. And since you've been good to me, you get to eat lunch today between noon and 1:00 pm. I know the First Lady will be happy that we're feeding you.*

With a big smile President Rizzo answered,

Thanks Maddie. Mrs. Rizzo thinks I've been getting a little thin these days. However, I think I fit better into my suits!

Without missing a beat, the seasoned secretary continued, *right after lunch sir you have a meeting with fifty Christian leaders you invited to the White House. With such a large crowd I scheduled the meeting for the Cabinet Room which can be expanded if necessary.*

President Rizzo thought for a moment and then said, *Sorry Maddie, I'm pulling executive privilege on this one. I want everyone here in the Oval Office.*

With a concerned look on her face Maddie countered, *Sir, it's going to be tight in here and I mean real cozy! I hope they're all friends!*

Looking out the window in his office, the president responded,

I'm not certain about everyone being friends but I am convinced they all share a common goal. I met most of them on the campaign trail and although I'm not in their spiritual league, their prayers and encouragement had a huge impact on the election.

They've come to pray Maddie--for me, the vice president, the Cabinet, other elected leaders, and especially the nation. Some are Roman Catholics, Pentecostals, and plenty of evangelicals. They've dropped their guard and have put away their doctrinal differences for the common good.

I don't know where you stand Maddie on the topics of God and faith but I want their prayers lifted-up from the Oval Office. We could all use a miracle or two!

Then with his signature smile brightening his face, the President added,

Oh. By the way Maddie, make sure the vice president and any other interested cabinet members are given an invite as well.

With a look of exasperation, Maddie Western headed for the door all the while thinking how they would squeeze everyone in.

And as if reading her mind, the Chief Executive chimed in,

We'll fit Maddie!

But even if we don't I'd like to go down in the history books as the first president to have a standing-room-only prayer meeting in the Oval Office!

Chapter 22

July 2017, Pyongyang, North Korean

North Korea carried out its first successful nuclear test in 2006--over four decades after the Soviets initially helped to construct the Yongbyon nuclear reactor plant in 1965. Despite the regime's normal subterfuge and saber rattling, Western intelligence sources affirmed four additional underground nuclear tests in 2009, 2013, and two in January and September of 2016.

The September 2016 test was the most powerful with an estimated yield between 10-30 kilotons. The resulting detonation created quite a seismic disturbance with a Quake Magnitude of 5.3 on the Richter scale. These *successes* were achieved internally and without outside help if one could believe the public denials of both the Russians and the Chinese.

Like seasoned card players, countries with nuclear arsenals typically hold their cards close to their chest. However, the Great Leader was one who played the game at his own table and by his own rules. And because of his iron grip on the nation, no one was quite sure how many bombs the North had. The best estimates were from twenty to sixty by the end of 2016. Furthermore, experts believed the regime had enriched uranium to make an additional six nuclear bombs a year.

*****

Perhaps it's human nature to avoid unpleasant truths! If so, that would explain the persistently low thresholds of success usually assigned North Korea's nuclear weapon and missile programs. For instance, shortly after underground test number four in January of 2016, experts downplayed the regime's ability to miniaturize warheads, a technological capacity necessary to fit nuclear devices atop missiles.

Interestingly, the general charged with defending U.S. airspace thought it *prudent* to assume that Pyongyang could indeed strike the U.S. despite the intelligence community giving it a *very low probability of success.*

It makes you wonder!

And what of the regime's boasting of backpack devices-- fact or fiction?

*****

In October of 2016, the Great Leader celebrated the 70th anniversary of the glorious founding of the North Korean Workers' Party with an unusual display. Interspersed between the rolling processions of North Korea's military might was a previously unseen infantry unit wearing rucksacks marked with the internationally acknowledged black and yellow radiation symbol.

A display with similar rucksacks had been first observed back in 2013. According to sources within North Korea, the Great Leader had challenged the nation's soldiers to become a *nuclear arsenal* in the event of attacks against the regime. With noted similarity to the kamikaze units that caused so much havoc before the closing days of the war in the Pacific, elite North Korean units would infiltrate the South and detonate their weapons.

Each rucksack was said to weigh between 22 and 62 pounds and worn like popular backpacks, a favorite of 21st century travelers. The weapons were not designed to recreate a Hiroshima or Nagasaki-type of explosive blast. Instead, the backpacks would create a horrific blast along with a plume of deadly radioactive material. According to one engineer, the radioactive contamination from such an explosion would prevent people from living in the blast zone for several decades.

A more frightening and crazy scenario could not be imagined-- unless you were the deranged leader of a completely totalitarian state! And now with a glowing rage, Kim Gun Suk had ordered select *volunteers* to transport not one but two backpack surprises to the residents of New York City!

The Great Leader's hatred towards the Unites States, fueled by the latest assassination attempt, focused itself on the pride of the Eastern Seaboard. There were many reasons to make the city a wasteland.

Economically, the infamous Big Apple nearly rivaled the GDP of the entire nation of Canada. Then the American upstart sitting in the While House grew up and lived in the city. Its destruction would inflict a grievous and long-lived wound! And then sitting beside the city's iconic harbor was the United Nations headquarters. Arrogant and full of petty chieftains, rulers, and sham artists, the institution had issued sanction after sanction against the regime.

Yes, there is no place on earth more deserving of our historic gesture.

Broadly smiling over his own clever plan, North Korea's ruler pushed a small button built into his desk. Within seconds a uniformed adjutant entered the room, located deep in a bunker considered safe from every threat to include a direct nuclear strike.

With a tone demanding absolute obedience Kim Gun Suk asked,

Have our special gifts to the Americans been released?

Yes, Great One! They were released immediately upon your orders and a special team had been assigned to oversee the transit to its West Coast destination.

And one of our newest submarines will be used?

Yes, sir. It is our quietest addition to our submarine fleet and one which the Americans know nothing about. It will deliver the special gifts unnoticed.

With a look of satisfaction, the Great Leader dismissed his underling and then turned his face toward the large world map on his wall.

He rose from his chair, stepped close to the map, and with a big smile placed his index finger squarely on New York City. Cocking back his thumb like the hammer on a revolver, he fired two imaginary bullets while quietly whispering *bang, bang!*

As he left the room he turned once more towards the map.

Goodbye New York City! Good bye!

Chapter 23

Mac's Naval Career & Family

Their six months in Florida's Panhandle provided Mike with a crash course in military life. Enlisted and officers exchanged salutes while warrant officers strutted about like protected species. Then there were endless lists of acronyms such as CVW or Carrier Air Wing, NAS for Naval Air Station; NAF for Naval Air Facility [was there a difference], and the one Mike particularly enjoyed, the MO or maintenance officer, and written as MOE. Quite quickly, Mac recognized that MOEs and enlisted maintenance personnel would become very important people in his career as a naval aviator!

After his last successful check ride, the next stop was NAS Kingsville for twenty-seven weeks of advanced strike training with over fifty graded flights. Mike's one-word description of this period of their married lives was simply s-t-r-e-s-s! But

Mac was both a determined and gifted flier and he completed his training in the top ten percent of his class.

He was then assigned to a Fleet Replacement Squadron for specific training on the F/A-18 where he earned his *wings of gold*.

In January of 1996, Mac received orders to a carrier strike group assigned to the 5th Fleet in Norfolk, Virginia. As a newly minted Lieutenant Junior Grade, he was ready to tackle the demands of a carrier pilot--but Mike was not ready for the cycle of ten-month deployments. Shortly after their arrival, they moved into a new apartment complex in Virginia Beach. Although it was seventeen miles from the naval station, it helped the couple--and especially Mike, escape the feeling of being swallowed up by military life.

Over the next eleven years of Mac's career, the couple bounced around from one carrier group to shore duty and back out to sea. During those *he's home* and *he's away* periods of their marriage, Mike managed to give birth to Jackson in 2002. Providentially Mac was there for the occasion before he shipped out again for a tour of duty in the Mediterranean.

The following year, she was not so fortunate. Grace, their second child named after Mike's favorite grandmother, came into the world soon after her daddy sailed off to fight in the Second Gulf War. A war that toppled Saddam Hussein's regime but which had many detractors who believed the U.S. should not have been there in the first place.

By the time her daddy, a highly decorated pilot soon to become a lieutenant commander, returned to home station, she was nearly one year old.

The fifteen years of navy life held a collection of bitter and sweet memories. Naval aviators were a tight knit group and the dangerous demands of the job made for lasting friendships. Spouses shared in this special fellowship with bonds not limited by location or shared assignments. Many of the relationships they enjoyed were built to last and especially with those who shared a common faith.

Although Mac had been raised in a Christian home and his parents walked the talk, his commitment to Christ was a mile wide and an inch deep. Finding himself in church most of his earlier years, he attended the youth camps, Bible studies, and most special events. Yet clearly, he did not have a relationship with God like Mike did.

Honestly, he was quite content to yield spiritual duties to his lovely wife while he handled the heavy lifting of naval life. Although he acknowledged answers to prayers and the uncanny accuracy of Mike's prophetic gifting, Mac remained a man with a self-orchestrated spiritual deferment.

And as Mike pressed into the Kingdom of God, time and again, the man of his life pushed out to sea. But one day that would all change and she hoped it would be sooner rather than later.

Chapter 24

25 November 2007, Kuwait City, Kuwait

Commander *Mac* O'Brien was enjoying forty-eight hours of shore leave in Kuwait City located on the southern shores of Kuwait Bay. It was a well-deserved break in an unrelenting sortie schedule tied to President Bush's famous troop *surge* announced earlier that year. The surge was in response to increasing sectarian violence in Iraq which by all rights had deteriorated into an uncontrollable civil war.

At home in the U.S. a clear majority of Americans disapproved of the war--a sentiment strengthened by a New York Times piece citing the Bush administration's failure to develop a comprehensive postwar plan for rebuilding Iraq. The Middle East had always been a tough neighborhood but events in Iraq had proven to have been in a league all by themselves.

As a flight commander, Mac was mentally and physically tired from the intense planning, the increased number of sorties, and in looking after his pilots which included a female Lieutenant who was new to carrier life. Consequently, he was not at all looking forward to returning to the hectic flight operations on the USS Dwight D. Eisenhower.

In a unique projection of U.S. naval power, the older Eisenhower had been joined by the John C. Stennis, the 7th Nimitz-class nuclear aircraft carrier in the Navy's inventory. No one could remember when two carrier battle groups had patrolled the warm waters of the Persian Gulf together!

Because of the war, deployments had been stretched and the Eisenhower was now in its seventh month abroad. Mac thought to himself, *just one more month buddy boy and you'll be home with Mike and the kids.* In his 15th year as a naval aviator, he was hoping to leave carrier life behind and find a stable commander job somewhere on solid ground. Although he absolutely loved flying--and especially his beloved F-18 Super Hornet, he deeply regretted the many months away from his family.

He knew things had to change.

I don't want my children to remember me as the dad who wasn't there for them. I've been the missing man in our family's formation and it's time that I took my place and helped Mike raise our kids together.

*****

Sitting in his hotel room facing the Bay, Mac checked his watch. He was seven hours ahead of Mike and the children in their home in Virginia Beach. Since it was Saturday, he didn't want to wake them too early and have a few grumpy campers on the other end of the line. However, at precisely 3 pm local time, he dialed his Skype cast call and settled into a comfortable arm chair near his bed. Several dial tones later he heard little Jackson's five-year old voice almost shouting,

Hello, is this you daddy?

Wearing a huge smile Mac answered, *you better believe this is your daddy and how's my number one son doing?*

I'm doing great dad and today Mom has promised to take us to the beach. I can't wait to jump into the water because it's been really, really hot here!

Mac thought about his two children who despite vastly different temperaments, both loved the ocean. If it was left up to Jackson and his sister Grace, they would both build a sand castle and then live in it. Moments later, Mac heard sounds of a long-distance skirmish as four-year old Grace demanded her phone rights.

Let me talk with daddy. You've had enough time. Mommy! Mommy! Tell Jackson to give me the phone!

Mac could just imagine the refereeing going on behind the scenes and just then, he heard Grace.

Hi Daddy. This is Grace. How are you doing Daddy! Are you coming home soon?

Thinking about his dark-haired beauty with a matchless pair of dark blue eyes, Mac answered his daughter.

Hello Grace and your Daddy is doing well but missing all of you terribly. And I can't tell you exactly when we'll be leaving here but it will not be very long. I promise.

Knowing his wife's morning rituals Mac asked, *Listen Grace has mommy had her first cappuccino this morning?*

Yes daddy and she's sitting here right beside me now. Do you want to talk with her?

That would be great my little princess--that would be great!

Waiting patiently as the family phone changed hands, Mac heard the lovely voice of the most beautiful woman in the world! With anticipation, he asked,

Mike, is this you?

Yes honey, of course this is me. Who else would be speaking with you at 8 a.m. on a Saturday morning! Oh Mike, I miss you so much…and I wasn't planning to say this but this deployment has been one of the hardest on me.

On the other end of the phone, Mac frowned as he quickly rehearsed their many separations sponsored by the United States Navy.

I'm so sorry Mike. Remember our conversation before I left? I've been in contact with officer assignments. Unfortunately, you understand the rules of engagement for our phone calls so I can't tell you much more than that.

I know Mac and thanks for telling me the little you could tell me. And as the dutiful wife of a Naval aviator, I know you can't answer the, when are you coming home question either.

No Mike but it will be sooner than you think. I can't wait to see you again honey. I think about you every day and I include you in every one of my prayers.

They continued to talk another twenty minutes with cameo appearances from little Jackson and Grace. Beach days demanded preparation and Mike needed to get the kids out of the house before the traffic rearranged their plans.

As they exchanged their goodbyes, Mike decided not to burden her husband with the details of an incredibly restless night culminating with an intense burden to pray for him. As the wife of a carrier-based naval aviator, she knew her husband lived in a particularly dangerous world. Over the years she learned that some burdens or intercessions could be shared while others were best prayed out before they were talked out or discussed.

The urge to pray for Mac's safety was so strong that she knew she would need the help of other prayer warriors as well. Picking up the phone Mike speed dialed a familiar number.

Hello Pastor Jim. Would you mind If I stopped by later today and if you don't mind, I'll have the kids with me. I don't want to appear mysterious but I have a terrible burden to pray for Mac and I could really use some prayer support.

Receiving an invitation to come by, Mike replied,

Thanks pastor and I'll stop by sometime after lunch.

Chapter 25

25 November 2007, Virginia Beach, USA

As Mike rode over to the pastor's home, she could feel the deep emotions rising up within what the Bible called her *inward parts*. It was in this innermost part of his being that King David often cried out to God for His help and mercy. She knew with a certainty born out of many years spent with God and His people that Mac was in trouble.

She had experienced times when her prayers, despite initially meeting resistance, would suddenly break through with a sense of victory or deep thanksgiving and praise to God. Sometimes her gift would operate and God would allow her to observe what was really going on behind the scenes. But in praying for Mac, she had neither seen nor heard anything at all! It was like pushing against an overwhelming darkness that refused to give up ground.

That is why she knew she needed others to join their faith with hers. It was Jesus Himself, who told the disciples in Matthew's Gospel,

If two of you agree here on earth concerning anything you ask, My Father in heaven will do it for you. For where two or three gather together as My followers, I am there among them.

Mike needed those who would agree and pray with her--and she especially needed the comfort of God's presence.

*****

Pastor Jim Davis and his wife Ellen had been swept up in the Jesus Movement in the late sixties. Pastor Jim was an outsized man with an equally large heart towards others. It was Ellen though who first got saved during a visit to her sister who lived on the West Coast. One night a bunch of ex-hippies began to share their God experiences at a local coffee shop. Ellen, whose marriage with Jim was falling apart, had flown out to California to clear her head and make new plans for her life.

She indeed cleared her head--and Ellen returned to Virginia Beach a new woman with a new agenda! A top priority was that Jim would likewise receive Christ. And though it took a year, when Big Jim fell, he fell hard for the Lord!

Together they've been leading their local congregation for nearly thirty years! They knew Mike quite well and loved and appreciated her humility and willingness to serve others in the church. They also recognized the hand of God on her life and her prophetic gifting. Pastors Jim and Ellen saw much less of Mac, especially as the tempo of Iraqi and Afghanistan deployments had increased, but they knew him to be a good man. They also knew that at times he had struggled with his faith.

Now as Mike and her two children pulled up to their home, the man and woman of God knew that this would not be an ordinary prayer meeting. Without being told the details, they both sensed that Mac O'Brien was in serious trouble--even danger.

But they would hear Mike's story and then, they would all pray.

Chapter 26

Antiquity Past

The prophet's servant arose early to begin his day in the company of a most unusual man. He had already witnessed his master perform many miracles in the name of Jehovah. There was a widow's jar of oil that remarkably flowed until all her debts had been paid. There was also a dead child who returned to life and even a foreign general healed of leprosy--that terrible wasting disease without a humanly known cure. The prophet's life was indeed one that bridged two worlds and two realities.

Stepping outdoors from their small dwelling located within the walls of the city, the servant looked towards the expanse of a brilliant blue sky cross stitched with small irregularly shaped clouds. He felt comfortable--and even safe in Dothan in its fortified elevation set among the hills of Gilboa. Stopping for a moment he thought to himself,

What a beautiful morning. I wonder what this day will bring as my master has been so unusually absorbed in his thoughts. Maybe he will reveal his plans but at any rate I will prepare breakfast and then wait for his arrival.

He then picked up an empty water jug and set off to a nearby well. Passing the main gate of the city, he noticed two clearly agitated guards making wild gestures with their arms. Placing the jug down, he raced up the stone staircase to quickly join the soldiers.

At first, his mind did not register what his eyes were clearly seeing. Circling the city were chariots, horses, and fierce soldiers carrying the standards of the king of Syria. Under the cover of darkness, a small army had encamped undetected around Dothan.

Within seconds, visual images gave way to a full- fledged panic as thoughts of capture, torture and even death assailed him.

They've come for my master, he thought! *I knew we would somehow get caught between the enmities of two kings. I must warn the prophet!*

*****

Finding his master sitting on the side of his bed, Elisha's servant flung himself at his feet. Looking up with a face of desperation, the servant described the enemy forces that lay in wait outside the walls of the city.

Alas, my master! What shall we do? What shall we do?

The prophet remained quiet for what seemed an eternity. Then extending his hand he gently lifted his servant's face towards him and said,

Do not fear, for those who are with us are more than those who are with them.

The words were measured, controlled, and spoken as if the prophet did not have a care in the world. Then shutting out the outside world, he entered the realm of heaven with a short prayer expressively for the benefit of his servant.

Lord, I pray, open his eyes that he may see.

Amazingly…the young man's eyes were opened to the supernatural realm!

Atop the mountains surrounding Dothan was another army, but this one was quite different! It was not an army of flesh and blood but one filled with horses and chariots of fire. Stunned by the sight, Elisha's servant could only shake his head in wonder. This man of God--the one he served daily could hear the secrets of a king and likewise peer into another world far greater and more powerful.

The prophet's prayer was simple, trusting, and directed to the God of Israel alone. The answer came immediately and with a suddenness that startled the servant into a new reality.

In an instant, the glorious flames of God obliterated the man's fears. He now understood his master's calm in the face of danger, his confidence in seeming impossible circumstances, and the joy he expressed when communing with his God.

His view of the life and the world he lived in would never be the same.

Chapter 27

July 2017, Beijing, China

President Rizzo's Asian trip had been downplayed by most media outlets and overshadowed by a list of contentious domestic issues. Some circles on the left, still smarting from the 2016 election debacle, continued to loudly beat the Russian conspiracy drum. Others who thought Rizzo's immigration policies and border wall between Mexico a horror, continued to protest around the country. Racial fissures, exacerbated by highly publicized police shootings involving minorities, continued to simmer and occasionally flare up grabbing national attention.

Yet the new president, whether you supported him or not, had in a relatively short period of time reestablished America's influence among the international community. His success with the Chinese was the latest case in point, and however unyielding Beijing had initially appeared, their reticence to reel in their North Korean neighbor faded into an American sunset.

Whatever one thought about one of the world's chief provocateurs, Kim Gun Suk was pragmatic enough to throttle back when faced with a dangerous curve in the road. It appeared that a sudden reversal of stance seemingly brought on by Chinese pressure fit into his plans quite well. A docile North Korea, willing to play by international rules, would further distance the regime from any kind of complicity when New York City succumbed to clouds of radioactive dust.

Providentially, Iran had upstaged events in the Far East with sponsored attacks on Israel and U.S. interests. Their religiously-fueled hatred of the Great and Little Satan's, terms originated by the Ayatollah Khomeini in 1979, drove their relentless efforts to join the elite club of nuclear powers.

The North Korean leader was almost ecstatic as he considered his good fortune. He knew the Ayatollah and his supporters had at least two nuclear backpacks, an initial delivery the Iranians were happy to pay a steep price for. Although transfer of the remaining four devices had hit a snag, he knew they would be willing to pay top dollar to get them into their hands.

The rotund dictator then summoned the head of Department 21, the North Korean cyber warfare agency, to his office. Within minutes the former director of Pyongyang's University of Automation and the nation's top hacker entered the room and stood at attention.

In a steely tone, Kim Gun Suk began.

I want you to leak to the Americans, British, and Israeli intelligence agencies scripted Iranian transmissions suggesting they've developed their own nuclear backpack devices.

With a questioning look the cyber chief asked,

But Great Leader didn't we sell them two such devices?

Of course, we did and to my knowledge there is no trail of evidence connecting us with the Iranian sale. In fact, we had our engineers design them to replicate Pakistani devices to further distance ourselves from the sale.

No, I want the Americans and her allies to seemingly trip over this information. Hack what you need to hack and cause them to dig a little. But I want them convinced that the Iranians have backpack nuclear devices and dirty bombs.

Acknowledging his new orders, the cyber chief replied.

Yes sir. I'll dedicate my top resources to this task. We have been very successful misdirecting the Americans and their allies before but as always, the Israeli's remain a more difficult challenge.

However, as you know anyone on the planet can be hacked!

Chapter 28

Scarsdale's Murray Hill-Heathcote area was credited with being the 14th richest neighborhood in the country with a mean family income slightly over $500,000. Famous residents Liza Minnelli and Linda McCartney joined the usual mix of old and new money. The city's founding father was Caleb Heathcote, an Englishman who lobbied to have his land recognized as a royal manor in 1701. After his death in 1721, the estate passed along to his daughters and by 1788 it was officially designated as a town.

In a marvelous twist of history, James Fenimore Cooper had based his novel, *The Spy* on the colonial town due to its prominent role in the American Revolution. Harvey Birch, the book's main character, was a common man suspected of spying for the British. How ironic that less than two hundred years after its publication, the town had other spies in the service of another foreign government.

James *Jimbo* Callahan and his wife Jin Lee were favorites among Scarsdale's country club crowd--he for his clever speech and infectious laughter and Jin Lee for her legendary graciousness as a host and sponsor of charitable events. She was also a raving beauty, with delicate Asian features, a petite figure, and gorgeous dark hair that trailed to her waist.

The couple met in 1990 during *Jimbo's* remote tour to South Korea. He had been assigned to the 51st Fighter Wing, Osan Air Base as an Air Force intelligence officer. Despite incessant requests to leave the military and work in the family's rapidly expanding fiber optics business, *Jimbo* simply wasn't ready. Then he met Jin Lee and fell head over heels in love with her.

She had been managing one of her father's two restaurants in Pyongtaek City, located four and a half miles from the Air Base, when the tall good-looking American came in and consumed enough food for two adults. He quickly became a regular customer and one day, Jin Lee agreed to go on a backpacking trip with him to Seorak Mountain. The scenery was breathtaking and it was there that *Jimbo* asked his Korean beauty to marry him.

The rest could be cited as romantic history except that…there was more to Jin Lee than met the eye.

*****

Years later, *Jimbo* discovered that his wife was a North Korean agent but after a brief struggle of emotion, love won out over patriotism. Her work at the restaurants had been a front allowing her to monitor base activities and cultivate a network of operatives. When told of the proposal, her superiors thought she had netted a prize in Major *Jimbo* Callahan, who not only came from wealth, but whose high-tech family business earned many classified military contracts.

Eight years later Lieutenant Colonel Callahan retired, having served the last two years of his military career as an intelligence officer for a three-star general assigned to the Pentagon. He then stepped out of an Air Force uniform in exchange for British-made Kingsman and Hackett tailored suits. His father was ecstatic with *Jimbo* working in the company and it wasn't very long before he took the reins along with a substantial salary.

The home in Scarsdale had been a strategic selection allowing for easy commute to the company's main manufacturing site in New Haven, Connecticut and for required travel to New York City's famed financial and banking centers. Longer trips to Washington D.C. or the West Coast were arranged with the company's small fleet of Lear jets.

*****

Life had been good for the Callahan's and until now their North Korean handlers had not required anything too risky of them. But tonight, they would open the massive gates to their mansion to special *guests* who would change all that.

With respect to the prime suspect in James Fenimore Cooper's historical novel, it was a classic *Harvey Birch* moment except that the alleged British spy had not been given two nuclear devices to visit untold destruction on a twenty-first century modern city.

Chapter 29

27 November 2007, Somewhere in the Persian Gulf

Commander Mac O'Brien forced himself to concentrate on the details of the mission brief featuring more close air action in Iraq's notorious Triangle of Death. Running south of Bagdad and sitting between Iraq's two great rivers, the region was known for its verdant surroundings, many farms and fields of palm trees. Yet beyond the pastoral settings raged a merciless kind of warfare in which Sunni's killed Shia's and Shia's returned the favor.

Despite a Shiite majority the area was a stronghold for Sunni insurgents--many of whom had fled U.S. military advances in the Anbar province. As an incentive to the combatants, monetary rewards were given to the faithful. Thrown into the mix were the Shiite militias who launched killing squads in retaliation for Sunni bombings.

It was a burning caldron of hatred stemming from age-old religious differences. However, both factions had one thing in common--they took extreme pleasure in killing Westerners and members of the Iraqi military!

*****

Below deck on the *Eisenhower*, the Mission Director concluded his briefing and to no one's surprise, it was another night mission in support of U.S. special operators. The destination was Al Hillah located 62 miles south of Bagdad and the capital city of the Babylon Province. Five kilometers north of the city of 300,000 plus souls were the ancient ruins of Babylon, prominent in the Bible for its seventh century conquest of Jerusalem and the people of Judah.

Regarding the great historical significance of the area, the single-seat F-18E Super Hornet was an excellent choice for their close air support role. The aircraft's eleven hard-point stations, loaded with JDAM precision-guided munitions [PGMs] would greatly minimize the possibility of collateral damage to non-combatants and the world renowned ancient ruins.

As the room was called to attention, Mac couldn't help thinking that he would rather visit the historic site rather than launch bombs against unidentified residents of the region. Turning to his two wingmen Mac quipped, *I hope you guys had your beauty sleep today. Looks like another late evening over the unfriendly skies of Iraq!*

*****

Hours later the three naval aviators rode a huge elevator bringing them up to the carrier's thousand-foot flight deck.

Overhead, a moonless sky produced a deep darkness punctuated by the lights of the *Eisenhower* and the thundering fiery red glows of jet afterburners. Winds were gusting at twenty to twenty-five knots which was a refreshing change from the stale air located below deck.

The carrier's heart and soul were found on its flight deck. Here men and aircraft performed a manic symphony delicately played out on runways which rose and fell with the ocean waves. Scores of sailors sporting different colored vests performed their dangerous assignments while interacting with pilots and flying machines that would soon be hurled out of catapults into the blackness of the night's skies.

Taking in a panoramic view of one of the Navy's most dangerous operational environments, Mac turned to his fellow pilots and said,

It's a thing of beauty isn't it! Controlled chaos intent on projecting American power to friend and foe alike!

Don't you just love it!

Still enjoying the ambiance, Mac looked for his assigned tail number, one of his favorite aircraft. Seeing a nearby plane captain Mac shouted,

Hey chief, where's my bird?

Sorry sir. We had to scratch 502 from the line-up due to a com-nav problem. Specialists are working it right now below deck.

That's okay chief. Everyone has their favorites and 502 happens to be mine. Looking up at his replacement Super Hornet, Mac asked, *any stories with this tail number?*

No sir. She's been a good plane. Had to take her out of the rotation for a scheduled engine change but she passed her functional check flight with flying colors.

Satisfied Mac replied, *Alright Chief! Let's get her ready then.*

*****

Mac pulled his last safety pin, waved it at the ground crew, and readied himself for the jolt of the catapult. In three seconds his aircraft would be screaming down the narrow runway at one hundred and thirty miles an hour. Once airborne it would take forty minutes to arrive at his destination.

Now high in the skies, Mac positioned himself as lead in the three-ship formation. As always, he whispered a prayer of protection and safety for himself and his pilots. Long before he had reconciled his role as an American fighter pilot and the destruction his aircraft could and would bring to others.

He remembered a conversation with his dad shortly after receiving his first carrier assignment.

Mac, God does not take pleasure in the death of the wicked but wickedness has its own unfortunate reward. Each of us will eat the fruit of our ways and God is free to choose the instruments of His justice.

Son, just make sure that you remain on the side of good and do your duty.

With that, Mac performed a radio check with his wingmen, slightly adjusted their flight coordinates, and then sped towards their target.

Mac's three-ship formation reached Al Hillah as planned after leaving the chaos of the Eisenhower's flight deck. He checked in with his two wingmen; both experienced pilots with plenty of combat sorties under their belts. The skies were pitch black as was the landscape surrounding Al Hillah's few flickering lights.

As the F-18s circled high above the target area, Mac thought to himself, *it's a good thing our guys have night vision goggles. It looks like one huge sheet of darkness down there!*

*****

The short 300 miles flight to Al Hillah was well within the 1,200-mile combat range of the Super Hornet. If required, this would allow for additional time over the target zone. The threat from surface launched missiles was low and with his PGM ordinance there would be no need to fly close to the deck. However, you never knew what to expect in a close air support role or what kind of trouble the special operators could get themselves into.

Twenty miles outside of Al Hillah, Mac connected with the air/ground controller embedded with the special ops unit.

Halo 33. Halo 33. This is your eyes on target. Do you read me?

Keying his mike, Mac responded.

Roger that ground eyes. We're circling twenty clicks away and enjoying the friendly skies. Have plenty of presents for your friends. Give me the coordinates and we'll deliver the packages.

*****

The first and second passes over the selected targets went without a hitch. Smoke and flames marked the remains of a compound used by Sunni insurgents to build deadly IEDs. Also gone was a cluster of military buildings, formerly used by the Iraqi army but recently commandeered by Al Qaeda. It would no longer be used to store weapons and stage raids. Both attacks though masked the special operator's real goal of capturing and/or eliminating local Shiite leaders of the Mahdi Army.

Their final pass of the night would create a firestorm of confusion and destruction which would help the good guys capture or eliminate the bad ones. Mac stayed in a holding pattern until the other two F-18s dropped their hardware. Then rolling his plane over, he began a rapid descent while toggling his armament stores. The altimeter read slightly below 10,000 feet when Mac heard a loud blast followed by a violent shuddering of his aircraft.

At first, he thought the unthinkable--that somehow the enemy had acquired medium range surface to air missiles. But there had not been a tell-tale vapor trail. Instead, his attention was riveted to his instrument panel which showed a completely disabled number one engine and a rapid loss of fuel in both wing and fuselage tanks.

Although Mac could not know it at the time, he had just experienced a catastrophic engine failure caused by a tiny piece of FOD [foreign object damage] picked up on the flight deck of the *Eisenhower*. A third stage compressor blade in the General Electric F414 turbofan engine was the first to fragment. Then the entire compressor disintegrated creating a radial path of destruction that tore deeply into the Hornet's fuselage. The aircraft began to roll violently and Mac's attempt to power out of it with his remaining engine failed.

The unthinkable was taking place as Mac fought to keep his plane from going down. The altimeter was furiously dropping and according to the book, Mac keyed his mike and called in one quick *mayday*. By then the damage from the exploding engine was so extensive that Mac no longer had any control of the aircraft.

The mortally wounded Super Hornet continued to hurtle towards the ground. Somewhere between 1,000 to 2,000 feet Mac managed to pull the D-ring of his Martin-Baker ejection seat and with a violent jolt, his chute deployed, and he was free of his aircraft. As he slowly descended Mac could see the glowing flames and destruction caused by his three-ship formation. On another day and in other circumstances, the sight might have aroused a sense of national pride and power. At that moment though Mac was feeling neither proud nor very powerful.

No! Commander Mackenzie O'Brien was frightened in a way that he had never experienced before.

Chapter 30

Τ he North Korean submarine program, considered a joke by some military analysts, consisted roughly of 70 subs, forty of which were *Shark-class* vessels built in the 1990s. Aware that many of their submarines were old and equipped with outdated technology a large chunk of the regime's military budget had been funneled into upgrading its fleet. Although Western intelligence had knowledge that the People's Republic had been developing a new nuclear *Gorae-*class of submarines, they did not know that the Sinpo shipyards had already turned out an operationally ready sub that was not only much larger than its predecessors but very quiet even by U.S. Navy standards.

The new submarine, given the name *Avenger* by the Great Leader himself, would slip out of its secret underwater berth and transport its special cargo undetected across the wide expanse of the Pacific Ocean. Similar in speed to the Russian *Akula*-class submarine, Pyongyang's latest threat to its many enemies would take a full eleven days to complete the 8740-kilometer trip to its destination, twenty miles north of San Francisco's famous Golden Gate Bridge.

Four grim faced special-forces soldiers were given the responsibility of guarding the bombs. Two other specially trained *detonator* troops were charged with training their American contacts on how to program and activate each backpack. If problems developed with their U.S. operatives, the *detonator* team would do the job themselves.

The mission must be a success. The Great Leader expected nothing less from his adoring followers.

Chapter 31

18 August 2007, Southeastern Syria

The door for martyrdom, which was closed by the end of the Iranian-Iraqi war, is now open in Syria.

Ayatollah Ali Khamenei, February 2016

I t went without saying that the Middle East was one of the toughest neighborhoods on the planet. Fraught by hundreds of years of religious, ethnic, and political animosities, the region was a perennial flash point for conflict--a truth Matthew Rizzo, former businessman and now America's chief problem solver had quickly discovered.

First there was tiny Israel faced with a continuing Hezbollah threat on its northern border with Lebanon, Hamas in Gaza, and a less than cordial Palestinian Authority in the West Bank. Beyond these enemies at the gates, loomed the much larger shadow of a radicalized Iran desperate to gain nuclear parity with their Jewish enemies.

Aside from Israel's valid defense concerns, thoughts of a nuclear Iran also sent shivers through the leaders of moderate Sunni governments in the region.

The president of the United States was now included in that club.

But aside from the ayatollah's race for a nuclear weapon, Iran presented another growing problem to the region. By using paid proxies, volunteers, and its own Revolutionary Guards, the *largest sponsor of state terrorism* extended its military influence into Syria, Iraq and Yemen. With over 200,000 troops, the so-called Liberation Army propped up Assad's forces and expanded its influence in Iraq while confronting ISIS fighters.

It also blurred the lines for the U.S., its coalition forces, and those backing the Syrian regime which also included Russia. Determined to reverse the perceived weaknesses of his predecessor, President Rizzo authorized the U.S. military to defend itself and its allies. Two consequential actions were taken which included shooting down a Syrian jet and the destruction of an Iranian drone launched against allied territory in southwest Syria.

These events brought the usual condemnations and threats from the Iranians and the Russians intent on expanding their influence in the region.

The Rizzo administration, despite its hard-liner image, was happy to let relations with the Russians and Iranians simmer down as no one wanted more conflict in the region.

And then it happened!

Call it an unintended act, a mistake, or the inevitable consequence of the fog of war.

Nevertheless, bombs were dropped, lives were lost and the wounded screamed for help--and once again, it was the U.S. military!

Chapter 32

18-19 August 2017, White House, Washington DC

I t was nearly midnight and the direct phone line from the Secretary of Defense began flashing. The president, fully awake and catching up on a stack of security briefs, answered.

Hello Mr. Secretary. I don't suppose you want to arrange a game of golf at this hour of the night?

The former four-star Marine general, an avid golfer, let out a quiet laugh.

No sir, Mr. President although the idea has some merit. Regrettably sir, I have some rather bad news to share with you and I was hoping to get to you before you read about it in the news outlets tomorrow morning.

By the way, I additionally coordinated with the National Security Advisor and he will arrange a meeting with the Principal's Committee.

The president braced himself for more bad news.

Well then let me have it Mr. Secretary--and both barrels please!

The SECDEF continued.

Sir, you recall that the Iranians have been poking their heads near our coalition forces in southeastern region of Syria near the Iraqi border. We shot down one of their drones and they raised all kinds of hell about it.

During the last five days, reconnaissance flights detected two armored columns advancing from different locations in western Iraq. We verified the recon photos with satellite imagery and concluded that most of the equipment was our own. Without HUMIT [human intelligence] assets on the ground, the on-scene commander concluded that the columns were ISIS units fleeing from a joint offensive by Iraqi and Iranian Revolutionary Guard forces.

Consequently, F-16 assets, forward deployed from their base at Incirlik, Turkey got tagged for the mission and...

Pausing to take a deep breath the SECDEF continued.

And sir, the fighters performed their job flawlessly but they were not ISIS columns. Mr. President, we wiped out two armored columns full of Revolutionary Guard volunteers!

Quietly the President asked, *were there any survivors?*

We think so sir but I can also tell you there were mass casualties.

Clearing his throat, the SECDEF went on,

Sir, there is one additional piece of bad news. Apparently, we took out Brigadier General Mohammad-Reza Zawadi, commander of the Revolutionary Guards' ground forces in the region.

President Rizzo remained silent for several minutes. Then collecting his thoughts, he responded to the SECDEF.

Thank you, Mr. Secretary! It's never easy to convey bad news and I'm certain that in your military career you've seen this type of thing happen before.

Yes sir. In fact, I've seen it all too often.

It looks like we've stirred an Iranian beehive. Well, there's not much I can do about it at this hour. I'll see you tomorrow morning at the Principal's Committee meeting.

Hanging up the phone, the president of the United States shook his head and sat down in his own leather recliner he had delivered to the White House. His thoughts became words spoken to an audience of one.

I can just imagine the Iranian response. It looks as if the Great Satan has given them all the ammunition they'll need. And to think that I asked for this job!

Chapter 33

25 August 2017, Near the Iraq-Iranian Border

*T*he American infidels must pay dearly for their high crimes against
The Islamic Republic of Iran! They have the blood of our sons on
*their hands. This vicious source of all the Middle East's problems has
driven a wedge among Muslims to prop up the cursed Israelis. They want
the world to forget Palestine but we will confront and destroy both these
enemies of Allah.*

*Yes, we will first make the Americans pay an exorbitant price for their
treacherous lies and the slaughter of our volunteers in Iraq. And know
this--Brigadier General Zawadi will certainly be avenged!*

*****

The American intelligence team at a secret Iraqi location near
the Iranian border dissected every word of the Iranian leader's
latest rant against the U.S. After rehearsing the speech a few

times, the station chief walked over to his two analysts who sat with headsets while glued to their large screen monitors. Aware that their boss was standing behind them, each man took off their headset while swiveling around in their chairs.

Well, what do you think, asked the man in charge?

The younger of the two analysts was first to offer an opinion.

I think it's just more of the same inflammatory rhetoric to keep the masses from realizing what a lousy life they really have in Iran. However, the hardliners in Tehran are probably eating it up and cheering the destruction of the Great Satan.

However, he did mention Zawadi by name but what the hell does that mean? I mean who was this guy that got the Ayatollah so fired up?

His older partner, one of the most senior Middle East analysts in the region, got up out of his chair and stretched his back. Turning to face his boss he added,

Who really knows what the Iranians are up too! I've been monitoring their communications for over twenty years and they still manage to surprise me. Mix together their political aspirations with Shiite end-times eschatology and you're left with a volatile package of irrationality that leaves me feeling like a meteorologist.

But since you asked Chief, here's my take. I don't know if Zawadi is dead or alive. But if we really did put him six feet under there will be some sort of a response--I can guarantee it! These people take vengeance to a new level.

The Station Chief nodded his thanks and said,

Let me know if you hear anymore chatter from our friends across the border.

In the mean time I'll fire this information off to Langley. It's nothing verifiable but I'm sure it will make someone's day for sure!

Chapter 34

6 December 2007, Virginia Beach, Virginia

The Notification Team consisted of a uniformed chaplain and an officer in the same pay grade as Commander Mac O'Brien. Theirs was not a happy assignment but each was a volunteer who wanted to do everything in their power to soften the blow to family members whose loved ones were either listed as Missing in Action [MIA] or Killed in Action [KIA].

Those with family members listed as MIA were left with a faint ray of hope that somehow their serviceman or servicewoman would be found alive. Tonight, the two-man team would not bring such hope for they would report to the woman with two small children that her husband would not be coming home.

*****

The night that Mac went down, his two wingmen had pulled up out of their dives and then climbed to a circling pattern at 15,000 feet. They then heard his mayday call and dove to the deck to find and assist their leader. Both pilots reported seeing a fireball followed by a larger secondary explosion which was almost certainly Mac's F-18. They continued flying over the crash site until two of the *Eisenhower's* Sikorsky SH-60 Seahawk search and rescue [SAR] helicopters arrived on scene. However, the SAR and rescue team were not able to land due to intense ground fire in and around the downed aircraft. Moreover, no one picked up a rescue beacon from the pilot which suggested that for whatever reason, he was not able to eject.

It took several attempts over the next few days before a Navy SEAL team could be flown in to secure the crash site. The area was flush with hostiles and the SEALs took a few casualties before they were ordered back on ship. Their conclusion: Without a rescue beacon, it was almost certain that the pilot rode the aircraft into the deck--and no one could have survived the crash. Reluctantly, the skipper of the *Eisenhower* agreed with the conclusions of those at the crash site and listed Mac as KIA.

*****

Arriving shortly after 7 pm, the grim-faced Notification Team walked up to the O'Brien's modest leased home and rang the doorbell. Mike, who had just finished the dishes after the family's evening meal, opened the door and instantly shuddered at the sight of the official car in the driveway and the two uniformed men now standing in front of her.

The Naval Commander spoke first. *Mrs. McKenzie O'Brien?*

Trembling, and with a fear that was crawling up from her stomach, she barely whispered, *Yes. I'm Commander O'Brien's spouse.*

The chaplain now spoke with a look of deep sorrow in his eyes,

Mrs. O'Brien, the Department of Defense and the United States Navy regrets to inform you that your husband crashed over Iraq and his remains were not found. A Navy SEAL team confirmed that his aircraft was down and that no one could have survived the impact. Gently he added, *your husband is not coming home ma'am.*

Mike felt as though the entire world had just collapsed on top of her as dozens of thoughts raced wildly through her mind.

What about the children? What am I going to tell them? How are we going to make it without Mac?

And then,

Why God? Why did this happen? I thought we had prayed through this Lord? I don't understand. How could this happen?

Having witnessed the scene on too many occasions, the chaplain softly continued.

Mrs. O'Brien, Commander Davis and I are truly saddened to have brought you this news. And as much as we would like to remove ourselves as reminders of your loss, there are important matters we need to share with you. May we go inside for a few minutes?

Unable to hold back the tears, Mike began to sob uncontrollably. By then her two children had made their way to the front door; witnesses to a scene that each would never forget.

Taking Mike's arm, the chaplain led the grieving wife and mother to a nearby sofa where they sat quietly while Mac's broken heart tried to reconcile the unthinkable.

With practiced silence, the chaplain sat quietly as wife and children grieved the loss of the man in their lives. He and his colleague would give the family as much time as needed before covering important details about death benefits and funeral arrangements.

Glancing over at his partner, their eyes locked in unspoken agreement both thinking the same thought, *this would not be a pleasant night!*

They never were!

Chapter 35

6 December 2007, Virginia Beach

The Naval Notification Team left the house shortly after 8 p.m., their unpleasant mission accomplished. Within forty-eight hours, a survivor assistance officer, would enter the picture to support the family in whatever way was possible. But that night as the team left, Mike closed the door and turned to face two very frightened children staring up at her.

Jackson, the older of the two, spoke first,

Mommy, what happened to Daddy and why were those men here?

And before Mike could answer her son, little Grace added,

Mommy why are you crying? I don't like it when you cry because it makes me feel sad too.

Mike struggled to find a way to respond; her emotions threatening to shut down all coherent thought. Then without a word, she took the hand of each child, sat down on the sofa, and hugged them both for a very long time. Silently she prayed,

Oh God, I can't believe that Mac is not coming home. Why did this happen and what am I going to tell my children?

There was no response from heaven…at least nothing that Mike could process, much less explain to her children. But some time later, the grieving wife regained enough composure to say the words no child ever wanted to hear.

Jackson, Grace, the men who came here tonight were from the Navy and they had very bad news about daddy.

Jackson immediately blurted out, *Mommy, what bad news about daddy? Did he have an accident? Is he alright?*

With hot tears streaming down her face Mike replied,

No Jackson. Daddy is not alright. His plane crashed somewhere in Iraq and… he is not coming home ever again.

The words were so final and incredibly painful to hear. Left in their wake, Mike and her two children wept, sobbed and clung to each other for well over an hour. Mercifully, sleep followed sorrow and Mike quietly carried each child to their beds. Gently kissing their foreheads, she stood and stared a long time at her wounded kids. She left each bedroom door slightly open, turned, walked down the hall to the room she had shared with Mac.

It had been a room full of laughter, intimate conversations, dreams, and the occasional anger brought on by some foolish treading on one another's *do not enter* zone. Now it would be no more than an empty space that was full of memories…

Totally spent, she eventually cried herself to sleep well after midnight. Just before dropping off, her mind kept repeating the same questions she had asked earlier.

Why? Why God? Why is Mac not coming home to us?

Whether she really expected God to answer her or not will remain unknown. But she did ask and He listened…and then The Almighty decided to answer.

*****

Mike awoke with a start…every cell, tissue and fiber in her body on high alert! She sat up in bed and wondered whether she was awake or dreaming. Then, in a pitch-black room, she sensed that she was not alone…someone was in the room with her!

Fear gripped her like a vise and it took all her courage to speak to the darkness.

Is there anyone here? Please tell me.

There was not a sound in the bedroom and she heard her own heart beating out a new and furious rhythm. Moments later, two events took place simultaneously: First, she heard a voice and then she smelled a fragrance.

Michelina I've come to answer your question.

The voice was pulsating with power and yet, it was gentle and loving. The words seemed to have increased the incredible perfume-like scent that had filtered into the room.

Her entire body trembling, Mike asked, *who are you?*

Immediately, she heard.

Michelina, you know who I am! We met in your Nonna's garden. Remember I saw you under your favorite tree!

Instantly the memory of her encounter with Jesus flooded her senses. Her entire being became revitalized and her heart began to skip and dance within her. An overwhelming feeling of love mixed with joy swirled around her.

Unable to hold back the words, Mike blurted out, *Oh Jesus, thank You for coming! I love You God!*

Still masked by shadows, Mike's Savior replied,

I know daughter. I know that you love Me! But tonight, I have come because You asked me a question from the depths of your pain-stricken heart.

You asked why Mac is not coming home to you.

Amazingly, the pain and deep grief Mike felt before falling asleep vanished in the Presence of the Lord. Now, Jesus' words reopened a wound that Mike thought would be impossible to bear.

Yes Lord! The night before his plane crash I had a tremendous burden for him. I felt as if he was in danger. I prayed with my pastors and it seemed as if we pushed through.

I don't understand God.

The greatest teacher mankind would ever know responded,

Michelina, I gave you the burden to pray for Mac. I put it in your heart to know he would face danger. But child you must always remember that while it is your privilege to pray and ask, I reserve the right to answer as I choose.

My ways are higher than yours and My thoughts towards you are for good and not for evil.

Swept by a rush of emotion Mike interrupted,

But Lord how could this be good for me and for our children?

Kindly Jesus responded,

I did not say such things would be good for you in the sense that you just described. They are good from My perspective for they accomplish My perfect plans for your lives.

Every man and woman will one day die and exchange the mortal for the immortal. Those who receive Me while on earth will live with Me in eternity. Those who reject Me during their stay on earth will be rejected by My Father in heaven.

Michelina remember I told you that your assignment on this planet would not always be an easy road but My grace would be there for you.

I told you that I will always keep you in My love. You can walk away from my provision but by trusting Me--even in this loss and whatever losses may take place in the future, you will prevail.

Like water cleansing out a wound, Jesus' words provided an antidote to Mike's pain and suffering. Rehearsing them over and over, she became convinced that somehow the family would make it and they would each go on with life.

Realizing that she had slipped deeply into her own thoughts, Mike peered into the darkness and called out to the Lord.

Only, He was gone.

What remained was a sweet aroma unlike anything on earth.

Chapter 36

January 2008, Virginia Beach

The past month had been an excruciatingly painful blur. Each day required a tremendous effort as Mike struggled to put distance between her shattered dreams and the unwanted reality of a life without Mac. On the other hand, the children, though visibly shaken by the tragedy, seemed to have weathered the storm much better than their mother.

However, it was just too soon to tell.

As the news broke, condolences flooded in from all over the country as relatives, friends, and the military community expressed their shock and sorrow. Immediately upon hearing the news, the pastors and members of Higher Ground church circled the wagons and provided the family much needed material and spiritual support.

Also, both Mike's and Mac's families drove the three hundred miles from Long Island to spend time with her and the grandchildren. It was hardest for Mac's parents and particularly for his dad, whose eyes told a story of utter devastation. For at least several days after their arrival, it was Mike who comforted her in-laws with a comfort she was surprised she possessed.

As the family continued its passage through its terrible nightmare, a strange thing took place. In the centuries-old Gospel account of the disciples crossing a storm-tossed lake, Jesus spoke to the raging winds and waves and chaos surrendered to calm. That same calm settled upon Mike, the children, and everyone close to them.

Doctrinal differences were set aside along with the view of those who wrapped death up in sad, hopeless boxes. Instead a crazy-kind of peace rolled up its sleeves and began working its way into hearts. Rivers of tears diminished to trickles and Mike pictured Mac not as one among the dead, but as a believer risen to everlasting life!

He was with the King of glory and as always, he was leading the way for his family towards a brighter future. Mike was also able to cast off the hammering thoughts that her prayers had failed to protect her husband. The freedom came when she handed over the outcomes of her praying to God.

The entire incident, although painful, highlighted the sovereignty of God in a new way.

A passage from the Book of Ecclesiastes strengthened this new perspective.

There was a time for every purpose under heaven: a time to weep, and a time to laugh; a time to mourn, and a time to dance...

Although Mike did not understand the *why* of Mac's departure, she knew she could trust God to rebuild her life and take care of her children. She would weep and she would mourn but she would also step back into life. There would be laughter again and there would be dancing.

*****

Surrounded by her parents, in-laws, and other close friends from New York, Mike realized that home was no longer in Virginia Beach. Consequently, she decided to have Mac, or whatever remains the Navy would supply, buried on Long Island. Afterwards, she would return to Virginia, pack up her household goods, and begin a new life in New York.

Arrangements were made at a funeral home near her parent's home. The showing would be followed by a military burial with full honors at the Long Island National Cemetery, a short ten-mile drive from Garden City.

As it turned out, if a funeral could ever be considered uplifting, it was Mac's. In fact, it was more of a celebration than anything else as speakers shared fond memories of Mac's wit, humor, courage and faith.

Disregarding tradition, Mac's parents left their seats to stand beside the head of their son's casket. There holding each other's hands, mother and father gave a tribute that only parents could give. Although there was not a dry eye in the place, the atmosphere was filled with hope and promise.

It was that kind of a funeral!

As the O'Brien's finished, Mike motioned to them to remain where they were. Then taking the hands of her parents, she led them next to her in-laws. Then two families became one, arm in arm, and heart to heart. Seizing the moment, Mike addressed the crowd urging them to follow suit.

And what happened next was more like a church service than a funeral. Later some would say they felt something like a cool breeze in the room. Others said they didn't feel anything and yet there were plenty of handkerchiefs present. In truth, it was a very bad day for mascara.

Some in the crowd received Christ as Lord and Savior. Others had their marriages and relationships healed. But to be certain, everyone left that funeral hall changed and with a little bit of heaven.

It was glorious---and yes, it was a funeral!

Chapter 37

16 Sept 2017, Lebanese Border with Israel

At precisely five minutes before midnight, thousands of Hezbollah fighters launched a barrage of short range missiles, mortars, and artillery shells across the Lebanese border into military and civilian targets in northern Israel. The date was chosen as a commemoration of Operation Badr which started the Yom Kippur War of 1973.

The bombardment completely caught the Israeli Defense Forces [IDF] off guard and it was the fiercest onslaught the tiny state of Israel had ever experienced. As one IDF officer put it, *the skies were raining death and destruction in a way we never could have imagined!*

In a coordinated offensive, Hamas suicide squads hiding in fishing vessels escaped detection by Israeli naval forces and landed near the coastal city of Ashqelon. With the help of collaborators, the Hamas terrorists waited until dawn before attacking public squares and shopping centers. Using hand grenades and automatic weapons they enacted a fearful toll taking the lives of over 50 innocent civilians with hundreds of wounded. All but one of the Hamas fighters had been killed by the IDF with an intense manhunt taking place for the remaining fighter.

*****

U.S. National Security Advisor Bill Brighton had his fingers laced behind his head as he leaned back in his chair to study the huge world map hanging in his office. Appointed just under ten months ago, he marveled how unstable the world had become—largely the result of previous administration's unofficial *hands-off* policies. President Rizzo's team had a huge challenge in front of them but at least no one believed that world peace would be achieved by tinkering with climate change.

No, he thought, *I think we're better off adopting some of Teddy Roosevelt's Big Stick ideas.*

Further musings were interrupted by a sharp knock on his door followed by a clearly concerned assistant. Without taking a seat, the bright young Harvard graduate with a PhD in International Relations cleared his throat and offered a brief excuse.

Sir, I'm sorry to barge in on you but I have some important but unpleasant information to share with you. I just got wind of it from the DIA and this is happening in real time as we speak. In an apparent coordinated operation Hezbollah and Hamas have attacked Israel. Hezbollah flexed its muscles using its restocked missile inventory while Hamas suicide teams attacked Ashqelon.

Holding up a hand, the Security Advisor asked.

What has been the Israeli response?

Not sure sir, the Prime Minister called an emergency meeting of the Knesset but we have no news yet. You know the typical Israeli response is more than an eye for an eye!

The assistant continued speaking.

Also, we do not have information on the casualties or the damage caused by Hezbollah's attack but we believe it is considerable. Both Hamas and Hezbollah claim their actions are in response to Israel's closing of the Temple Mount back in July. You know how most of the Muslim world went off the rails over that.

Then the young man stopped his narrative and said to his boss,

Sir, there is one more thing.

Brighton asked *more bad news?*

I'm afraid so sir. Less than an hour ago, the guided missile destroyer USS Laboon was severely damaged by a mine in the Strait of Hormuz. She was operating well within the two-mile median required of the Traffic Separation Scheme. Just twenty-four hours before the incident, the 5th Fleet's minesweepers had worked those specific coordinates in the Strait.

Angrily Bill Brighton stood to his feet and demanded.

Then how the hell did this happen?

165

Sir, I'm not a CIA or DIA analyst and you know my dissertation focused on the broader effects of Islamic fundamentalism in the Middle East and not with special reference to Iran.

Moreover, I'm not a betting man--and never have been, but I would put a big red pin on those wide-eyed folks in Tehran! They probably used their fast boats or even a sub to mine the shipping lanes after the Navy had swept the area.

Taking a deep breathe the nation's Security Advisor sat back in his chair slapping the desk with both hands.

That's just great and it's all the President needs to hear right now. If it isn't the Koreans, it's the Iranians! What a crazy planet we all live on.

Anyway, I'm going to personally deliver the news to President Rizzo and then watch the fireworks!

His assistant shrugged his shoulders, turned to exit the room, and added,

Good luck sir! I think you'll need it.

Chapter 38

20 Sept 2017, Moscow, Russian Federation

The Russian President sat perplexed rolling over in his mind the contents of the dossier sitting on his desk. Finally, he hit his intercom. Answering immediately, his aid replied: *Yes, Mr. President.*

In his customary brusque manner, the wily former KGB operative, demanded,

Get in contact with General Babikov. I want to see him in my office as soon as possible.

General Valetin Babikov was head of the most important intelligence agency in the Russian Federation. Its official name was the Main Intelligence Agency of the General Staff of the Russian Armed Forces but more commonly it was known as the GRU. The general had an illustrious military career dividing time between Spetsnaz Special Forces and various intelligence units. He was known to his subordinates as a harsh and unforgiving man and someone you would never cross. Standing at six-foot four, the sixty-two-year Colonel General still carried himself like a commando.

*****

An hour later, Babikov entered the office of President Ivan Puzakov who without a word motioned the general to the chair in front of his desk. Although neither man considered friendship a valuable commodity, they shared a mutual respect born out of the many dangerous gambles both had been willing to take over the years.

Understanding that the President's request had been urgent, the general cleared his throat and broke the silence.

Comrade President I came as soon as I could.

While continuing to look at the file on his desk, President Puzakov asked,

What are the Iranians up to?

Pausing a moment before answering, General Babikov was wise enough to avoid parroting back a summary of the intelligence report Puzakov was undoubtedly reading.

The Iranians excel in their little intrigues. I have no doubt their Hezbollah and Hamas vassals were prompted by Tehran to launch their so-called punitive strikes against the Israelis.

Looking up from the report, President Puzakov questioned,

And what about the American destroyer in the Straits?

The head of the GRU continued.

Based on our sources, the Iranians have somehow gotten their hands on a new quieter sub or subs sophisticated enough to escape American sonar detection.

Puzakov responded with another question.

Where could they have gotten such a sub? Could our Chinese friends be involved?

Without emotion the head of the GRU replied.

No sir and this is my assessment only: I believe they got them from the North Koreans.

With a look of surprise Puzakov asked,

The Koreans! I didn't think they were anywhere close to building sonar escaping submarines--and especially anything that could avoid detection from the U.S. Navy!

The general added,

The little man in Pyongyang may appear a bit deranged but he understands the game very well. I have dedicated additional resources to investigate what the North Koreans are up to. However, my view is the Iranians have acquired super quiet subs and that is very bad news for the Americans.

Shifting back to the recent attack on Israel, the Russian leader asked a few additional questions.

What has been the Israeli response to these attacks?

With a sudden grin Babikov answered,

As you would expect! The Israeli's are exacting their usual punishment just short of an all-out invasion. As we speak, the IAF is attempting to bomb Hezbollah back into the Dark Ages. In Gaza, there will be hell to pay as well but for now the Israelis are taking on the greater of the two threats.

Then what about the Americans? I'm sure the new U.S. leader is enjoying this sudden baptism into the Middle East's treacherous currents.

The General's grin grew larger as he responded,

This will be the first of many tests Rizzo will face. His military is worn out from too many conflicts spread out over too many years.

Politically the Democrats and the media are waging their own war against him. Not to mention accusations that we somehow helped him win his presidential campaign.

And finally, the ayatollahs are committed to their eschatological delusions...and that, adds a deadly element of unpredictability to everything they do.

Consequently Mr. President I suspect your American counterpart would probably wish that he had never left his successful business ventures!

Chapter 39

T he rented Lexus GX 460 full sized luxury SUV was perfect for the long trip from the West Coast to New York's Westchester County. As planned, it had taken a leisurely six days to drive the twenty-five hundred miles from California to the front gate of the Callahan's Scarsdale residence. As part of their cover, they had three planned business trips; all on the way back from their drop in New York.

The two casually dressed North Korean agents were part of the regime's strategy of staying close to their enemies. They were both mid-level managers employed with a successful Silicon Valley start-up computer company specializing in security software. Of course, other companies lacked the competitive advantage that Fail-Safe Computer Solutions had, especially as some of the world's best hackers secretly worked for the company across the Pacific and north of the 38th parallel.

And despite their almost jovial demeanors, each man was a lethal package complete with the requisite skills of a spy...and when needed, an assassin! During the road trip, the team never removed their *packages* from their vehicle staying with the SUV in shifts when spending the night at hotels. They were now happy to deliver the goods, rehearse the planning, and provide instructions on placement and priming the *packages* to go live when scheduled.

*****

Using a pay-as-you-go phone, the man in the passenger seat sent off a brief text message. Twenty seconds later, the gate swung open and the SUV followed a long and winding tree-lined driveway to the 10,000-square foot mansion. A tall man and his Asian wife stood waiting at the front door. They would be alone for the night. As a token of their appreciation, the couple had given the entire staff the weekend off.

Pointing to the five-car garage, the tall man activated the overhead door and the SUV slowly pulled in. The couple then walked over to the Lexus and closed the garage door behind them. The *packages* were carefully removed from the back of the SUV and then brought into the couple's safe room, expertly hidden behind a wall in their huge bedroom.

Their most important mission was ahead and though it was far more than they had bargained for, they knew the ground rules very well. Assignments from Pyongyang were to be carried out. There would be no questions and absolutely no room for error.

To fail was certain death…a fact that wonderfully motivated the husband and wife to listen to every word of instruction from their new guests

On the other hand, if they were to succeed, many, many people would lose their lives.

Just another set of contradictions so common on Planet Earth!

Chapter 40

March 2008, Oceanside, New York

I *need to take the children and go home to be around family. This is not a time to brave things alone.*

Like a recording, Mike's internal dialogue had been playing all morning.

I'll miss pastors Jim and Ellen and the church but Jackson and Grace need the love of their grandparents. I need it as well.

It wasn't an especially difficult decision to make since both sets of parents were eager to have the family near them on Long Island. Mike knew the area and although it was expensive, Mac's financial planning gave her the option to live just about anywhere. Another important consideration was the beaches which always proved a tonic for her soul. She absolutely gloried in the sun, surf and sand as did her children.

From the time each could waddle down to the water's edge, Jackson and Grace would morph into adorable fish sporting arms and legs instead of flippers. With a smile Mike concluded,

Yes, we'll need beaches as well.

As she sorted through the estate, Mike became very thankful for Mac's planning for the unthinkable. On many occasions, he offered to rehearse the details with her, but she found the topic too morbid a subject.

Okay Mac. I appreciate all the planning but you're not going anywhere. And if God does decide to take one of us, I'm going first.

Remember ladies always go first!

Amused by her theatrics, her husband would table the discussion adding his own well-worn disclaimer:

You can't say I didn't try Mike but if, and only if, I checkout before you, the important documents are here in our safe.

The memory triggered a wave of pent up emotion as tears, sobs, and deep groaning took over. Mike began rocking back and forth with an acute suffering not explainable, but only felt at the deepest and most intimate realms of the human heart.

She was hurting and the pain would remain with her for some time. Yet, one day there would be closure. One day, God would help her heart to find healing.

*****

It took several months after the funeral to terminate her lease, find a house in Oceanside on Long Island's south shore, and close out their lives in Virginia. She felt especially excited about the remodeled Cape Cod house she practically stole for slightly under $400,000. The two thousand square foot home was located on Hull Street, a shady lane, adjacent to Foxhurst Road. It had an open floor plan, a remodeled kitchen, and two upstairs bedrooms separated by a single bathroom. The bedrooms would be perfect for Jackson and Grace although the solitary bathroom would become the site of frequent adolescent conflicts!

Less than seven miles to Garden City, Mike was close--but not too close to her family and in-laws. Everything fell into place and there was much thanksgiving for finding a house in such a great location. Mike treasured the look on her realtor's face when she wrote out a bank draft for the entire amount of the sale.

Later, the Navy retrieved her household goods from storage and delivered them to her new address. The carrier unpacked everything and placed furniture and boxes wherever Mike wanted them to. It was a seamless process that she had become accustomed to throughout their military assignments.

As the moving van drove off, Mike realized her previous Navy life was over. It was time for old things to pass away and for new things to come. And that included the work of Mike's hands and heart. She had the children to rear and it would be another twelve to thirteen years before they walked out of her door to their respective universities and careers.

Despite it all, Mike remembered that she had been marked for good with the Lord Himself appearing to her on two occasions. With use of a heavenly stylus, His words were forever etched into her heart,

I have chosen you to serve and love My people...I will open your eyes to see My kingdom and to hear My words. You will see and hear things that others will not see or hear. Your gift will make a way for you to go before great men.

This assignment will not always be an easy road but My grace will keep you.

My grace will always keep you in My love.

Yes, Mike would do her very best to love, train, and launch her children into their destinies. But she would also pursue her calling.

Chapter 41

Summer 2009, Oceanside, New York

At just after seven in the morning Mike tossed her blanket down at her favorite spot at Jones Beach. Normally she would have taken the kids but she had arranged to have them stay with her in-laws for the day. She needed beach therapy and Jackson and Grace always enjoyed their time with Grandma and Grandpa O'Brien.

In a couple of hours though the world-famous park featuring over 2,400 acres of beautiful white sand and surf would be overrun by a mass of humanity. At that moment though Mike and the other early risers had the beach to themselves. As she walked down to the chilly waters of the Atlantic Ocean, she mentally patted herself on the back with an old cliché:

The early bird gets the worm and smiling she added, *and I get the beach all to myself!*

Standing at water's edge, she watched as set after set of three to four-foot waves crashed on shore, each one sending an advance guard of surging, foamy water up to where she stood. With the rising sun warming her face, she steadied herself against the pull of the receding waters by digging her toes deeper into the wet sand. Looking down at her feet she thought,

Yup, I'm stuck in wet sand alright.

It seemed that no matter how hard she tried to move past Mac's death, her own misreading of the events with the sensing that all was well, continued to haunt her.

How could I have been so wrong? I was convinced that God would protect Mac from whatever dangers he had been facing.

How can I rely on my so-called gift if I completely missed it with the most important person to me on the planet? I can't do this. I can't pray, see or hear for others if it doesn't work for me.

Overhead, she looked up at two circling seagulls effortlessly soaring upon the morning's on-shore winds. With eyes veiled by self-criticism and uncertainty, she continued in the court of accusation.

And why couldn't God rescue Mac? After all, I asked and I pled my case before Him just as He told me to.

What happened to Psalm 91--with long life I will satisfy him?

Tears began to well up and Mike became so lost in her sad story that at first, she didn't notice a young mother holding a newborn baby a few feet away. However, looking around she caught the eyes of the woman who responded with a faint smile. Mike could tell though the effort was a sacrifice which arose from a desperation so thick you could almost touch it.

The girl could not have been more than seventeen or eighteen years of age but she already bore the mark of a much older woman's pain and rejection marring the natural beauty of her face. It was her eyes though, the windows of the soul that reached out to Mike, pleading for some hope and a human touch.

Mike averted her gaze, turning back towards the shore break with its unrelenting assault of the beach. Her heart wanted to talk to the woman, take her hand, and in some way help ease her pain but...she had nothing to give.

Before Mac's death, she would have welcomed the opportunity to share the good news of a God who would willingly love the mother through the dark night of her soul. That was before.

Today she would settle the matter differently!

There's no way! I can't really help her. My prayers and gifts missed the mark when it really counted. I'm sure she can find someone else who can help her with her problems.

Then without a word, Mike turned and walked back to her blanket. The sun was brilliantly rising and she stretched herself out on the warm sand. For the next few hours she would shut everything and everyone out of her world.

Everyone!

*****

By noon, Mike had enough of the crowds so she packed up, got on the parkway, and headed home to Oceanside. At the house, she had a full plate waiting with errands to run, plants to repot, and both the kid's rooms desperately needing a mother's touch. Later she would swing by and pick up Jackson and Grace at her in-laws.

All in all, the beach had helped to relax her and shake off a few stressors. However, she kept thinking about the young lady with the baby but there was nothing she could do about that now. The opportunity had been lost, tried in a court in which the final verdict read,

Not available--find someone else!

Interestingly, birds who for whatever reason lose the ability to fly continue to look up to the skies above. Yet in Mike's case, not only had she stopped flying but she had also stopped looking up.

Until something quite terrible happened!

Chapter 42

The next day, Oceanside, New York

It was a bright, sunny, muggy day on Long Island with temperatures in the low nineties but the humidity off the charts. Like Charles Dickens' famous line, it was the best of times [for those indoors or in cars with air conditioning] and the worst of times [for everyone else without AC]. But they needed to eat and so Mike took the children with her to Trader Joe's for groceries.

Although not a daily newspaper reader, the Long Island Press had a huge feature on the 29th Olympic Games in Beijing, China which interested her. She picked up a paper at the checkout, herded her kids to the car, and put the groceries in the back of her two-year old Lexus SUV.

She then hurried home, made lunch, and let the kids swim in the pool for several hours before her pastors came over for a visit. Kyle and Diane Hanson had co-pastored *The Abiding Church* since its unorganized, unaligned, and spontaneous inception in 1972. Kyle and Diane would often say that God ran out of trained ministers so He picked up a couple of hitchhiking hippies to start a church with.

Mac attended the church along with his parents during his time on Long Island. During their marriage, whenever the family had been to the Island they would visit the church and enjoy the dynamic worship, preaching, and moves of God's Spirit. The Hanson's were genuine no-frills people who loved God and were not afraid to show it and live it. They also had very powerful prophetic gifting which was one of the reasons Mike felt so comfortable there.

Ever since Mike and the children moved back, the Hanson's had made themselves available to the family. They were never pushy and they gave Mike plenty of space while continuing to pray in between the gaps. She was forever grateful for their help and Mike knew she could count of them for just about anything.

They would arrive in an hour and Kyle would expect a deep dark espresso while Diane was content to just sit and chat. After preparing a tray of fruit, cheese, and crackers, Mike checked on the kids and sat down in her favorite chair for a few minutes. Picking up the Long Island Press she scanned the frontpage headlines and flipped through to the back of the first section for more information on the Olympics. Halfway down the last page, in a small two column article, was a headline which read, *Tragic Drowning at Jones Beach.*

Mike's heart began to pound as she read through the first lines of the piece.

Yesterday afternoon lifeguards stationed at the western end of Field Two recovered the bodies of a young woman and an infant from the turbulent waters of the Atlantic Ocean. The apparent mother of the child was fully clothed and although a coroner's report is pending, she appeared to have been between sixteen to nineteen years of age. The baby was not more than several months old.

State police are investigating the deaths and have not ruled out the possibility of suicide...

With a gut-wrenching sob Mike slid off her chair and fell to the floor. Her wailing was so loud both children came rushing in from the family room. With worried looks on their faces, Grace was the first to ask,

Mommy, what's wrong? Why are you crying like this?

Curled up in a fetal position, Mike could only mutter,

Oh, God. I am so sorry--I am so very sorry! I didn't say anything, I didn't care enough.

The children stood quietly by as their mother repeated over and over the same broken words of regret. At that point the bell rang and Jackson raced to the front door. He fumbled with the lock but soon managed to open only to find pastors Kyle and Diane staring back at him. Noting the alarmed look on his face, Diane asked,

Kyle, what's wrong?

At that point, they both heard the most wretched sounds coming from inside the house. Kyle then pointed towards the kitchen and said,

My mom is crying and we don't know why.

Finding Mike on the floor Diane sunk down and cradled the grieving woman in her arms. Kyle began praying as Mike continued to moan,

I'm so sorry God...I'm so sorry!

*****

Long ago Israel's king recorded his dealings with a merciful God in words that only the broken hearted can really appreciate. David's failures as a ruler and man ran deep and wide--in fact, far deeper and wider than he could hope to recover from. Yet he discovered a truth about God that simply overwhelmed the soul: The Lord Almighty will not reject a broken and contrite heart. Through His Son, He is willing to forgive the deepest and darkest of sins.

And that night in Oceanside, a broken woman was pulled up out of her dark pit to receive the rich and undeserved gift of forgiveness.

It was incredible and it was beautiful!

But there was more!

Those who are forgiven much and recognize the tremendous price paid to obtain their forgiveness, also love much!

Mike was now ready to live and she was ready to love!

Chapter 43

M *r. President we can't let the Iranians get away with nearly sinking one of our ships in the Strait of Hormuz!*

The SECDEF's neck bulged and his face was the color of a bright red tomato. The former Marine general was not known for turning the other cheek and he was absolutely unbending in making any concessions at all with the ayatollahs.

The Vice President added his support for taking a hard line while others in the Cabinet cautioned restraint. As Matthew Rizzo listened to the nation's best and brightest, he kept thinking about Harry Truman's famously quoted sign that sat on his desk--the buck did indeed stop with the president. Right or wrong whatever decision he would make--or not make, would become a matter for the history books. But the former businessman had spent most of his adult life making crucial decisions which against all odds had landed him in the Oval Office.

Clearing his throat, the President interrupted the spirited debate raging around the table.

Ladies and gentlemen, I appreciate your analysis, insights and diversity of positions on the topic of a response to Iran. I'm the new guy on the block and I do not claim any type of military prowess or a special understanding of Middle East dynamics. However, I think you would all agree with me that the region has been a deep pit of sectarian violence and intrigue for many centuries.

But understand that the American people elected me to protect the nation from all enemies foreign and domestic. I am also a New Yorker and we do not take crap from anyone. If Tehran thinks they can run the U.S. out of the region then they have seriously underestimated me and the resolve of the American people.

This hasn't been the first time that Iranian attacks have taken the lives of Americans.

The Secretary of State, a straight shooter who spoke his mind freely, interrupted the president.

Excuse me Sir. I don't want to overstep my boundaries but please bear in mind that the Iranians are reacting to our bombing of their Revolutionary Guard volunteers. We started this fistfight!

Pausing a moment to take in the Secretary's words, the nation's leader responded.

Thank you Mr. Secretary and I want you to always take the liberty to challenge my assertions and to state your views. I didn't hire anyone here to be a yes man or a yes woman.

I do want you to know that I have considered your views but I'm painting a larger picture here. We all know that the regime has been undermining the Middle East for years. They've armed their surrogates in Lebanon and in Gaza and no thanks to former administrations they are hell-bent on building a nuclear capability. I remind you, in the ayatollahs view; we are the Big Satan while Israel remains the Little Satan.

I didn't draw any lines in the sand when I came into office.

Then the President peered directly into the eyes of every person in the room.

And I'm not going to waste my time drawing one. However, it's time we clamped down on the Iranians and I mean good and hard.

Turning to the SECDEF, President Rizzo said,

We're going to DEFCON 1! I want our nuclear arsenal placed on its highest alert.

Hardly masking his shock, the Vice President questioned,

Sir, the nation has never reached DEFCON 1 before. The closest we ever got was DEFCON 2 during the Cuban Missile crisis.

I know Bill, believe me I know! The Chief Executive continued.

But we'll see how the Iranians react when they realize that 1,500 strategic nuclear devices are pointed in their direction.

Then turning back to the Secretary of Defense the President added,

I also want a second carrier group in the Persian Gulf. And get word to the Iranians that if any--and I mean any, threats or provocations are

made against our ships in the Strait of Hormuz there will be an immediate response.

With that the leader of the Free World turned and exited the room.

Chapter 44

1 Oct 2017, Touching the apple...

Moshe Bar-Lev was Chief of the General Staff of the IDF and he was faced with the problem of dealing with yet another crippling attack by Hezbollah on its northern border with Lebanon.

In 1982, Israel had invaded southern Lebanon to put a stop to repeated attacks by Yasser Arafat's Palestinian Liberation Organization fighters. That offensive effectively ousted the PLO as well as Syrian forces from Lebanon and helped to install a pro-Israeli Christian government with the promise of *forty years of peace*. At the time, Bar-Lev had been an untried Second Lieutenant assigned to the famed Golani Brigade. The fighting was fierce and he lost men--and the peace never happened!

From 1985 to 2000, southern Lebanon and the Israeli border endured repeated attacks by Iranian-backed Hezbollah guerrillas. During this period, the IDF also contended with a First and Second Palestinian Intifadas which heightened tensions in the region to a fever pitch. Then in 2006, Hezbollah abducted two Israeli reserve soldiers sparking yet another all-out war in Lebanon. Despite taking a severe pounding by the combined air and ground strength of the IDF, Hezbollah survived, with enough breath remaining in the organization to live and fight another day.

That day had come and it came with a vengeance.

Yet what most people outside of Israel did not realize was that the IDF was largely an army of reservists comprising over seventy percent of its listed strength. Every call-up of reservists deprived the nation of its doctors, engineers, businessmen, and blue-collar workers who fueled the economy with their skills. Due to the continuing crisis, Lieutenant General Bar-Lev saw no other option but to ask the Minister of Defense for a recall of 125,000 reserve forces. That decision would prove costly but the IDF was dealing with a vastly more lethal enemy armed with Iran's most sophisticated short range and medium range rockets.

It was during the 2006 war that large Israeli cities had first come under attack by Hezbollah missiles and rockets. That led to the development of a multi-layered air defense system featuring Iron Dome, Arrow, and David's Sling batteries. With an interception rate of eighty-five percent, Iron Dome system had proven itself well against shorter range rockets while the more advanced Arrow and David's Sling batteries addressed threats from medium and long-range missiles. In 2016, both Arrow and David's Sling aerial defense systems had been deployed.

But as Bar-Lev pondered his intelligence reports, he realized the issue was one of volume and not efficiencies. With over 100,000 various sized rockets and missiles in Hezbollah's arsenal; most missiles had been intercepted and destroyed. However, the terrorist group was scoring hits on civilian areas deep within Israel--and that was entirely unacceptable!

Reluctantly, Bar-Lev knew an invasion with ground forces was needed to rid the nation of the hornet's nest to the north. Hezbollah and its rocket attacks had to be stopped now.

He also acknowledged that Israel would eventually have to do something about Iran. Of that he was quite certain--and with or without the help of the United States!

Chapter 45

I n the year that King Uzziah died, Isaiah saw the Lord sitting on a lofty throne and His robe filled Heaven's Temple. Above the throne were seraphim--powerful and majestic angels, who continually cried out,

Holy, holy, holy is the Lord of hosts; the whole earth is full of His glory.

Their voices shook the Temple to its foundation, and the entire building was filled with smoke. As for the prophet, he had seen with his own eyes the King, the Lord of all angel armies, and he was undone. Reduced in his humanity and all too keenly aware that he was in the presence of a holy God.

Then there was Ezekiel the priest who had been carried into captivity by King Nebuchadnezzar of Babylon. On one seemingly ordinary day he sat among his countrymen beside the River Chebar. Suddenly the heavens were opened and he saw many detailed visions. More importantly, Ezekiel saw God and the experience changed him forever.

Why do some see the invisible and meet the indescribable? No one really knows except God and He is not required to tell!

In moving over to the New Testament, John the Baptist saw the heavens opened and the Holy Spirit descend like a dove upon Jesus. He also heard a voice from heaven saying,

This is My Beloved Son, in whom I am well pleased.

Later after Jesus has ascended and the Day of Pentecost had come, those in the Upper Room all heard a sound from heaven and all saw tongues of fire alighting upon those who had gathered. The momentous event shook the natural world as the Holy Spirit began taking children of faith deeper into the supernatural realms of the Kingdom.

God alone holds the keys to His Kingdom. Those privileged to see and hear beyond the constraints of the natural world, do so for His good pleasure and eternal purposes.

It is always for His good pleasure and eternal purposes!

Chapter 46

2010…Long Island, New York

Those who knew Mike since she returned to the Island were amazed at her remarkable transformation! Gone were the dark clouds, the lingering sadness, and the gaping holes in her spiritual armor. Those closest to her benefited the most as her entire focus shifted outward, seeking to bless others with her time, talents, and spiritual gifts.

Life still had its challenges and there wasn't a day she didn't think about Mac and their lives together. But she had a revitalized faith which enabled her to view the world from a heavenly perspective. Each day was a gift, pure and simple. She would honor Mac's memory by living well and in the full light of God's calling.

Her pastors, who were always fond of the couple, took a special interest in Mike and her prophetic ability to see and hear from the spiritual realm. On her end, Mike learned a great deal from the church's prophetic school which met regularly throughout the year. The curriculum, developed by her pastors, took an in-depth Bible-centered look at the subject which completely fascinated Mike.

Other speakers added their own rich perspectives on the spiritual gifts and the five-fold ministry offices found in the fourth chapter of Ephesians. Best of all, the school provided an opportunity for people to exercise their gifts in a safe, supervised setting.

Mike discovered that while all believers could prophesy and speak edification, encouragement, and comfort to others, not everyone had the ability to step into the supernatural realm or receive insight from God on future events. That was the Spirit's business pure and simple. But for those with such callings, a key was to avoid pitfalls of pride and deception while maintaining a humble heart and intimate relationship with God. Mike discovered that a daily intake of the Bible and much prayer kept her soul limber and free to respond to the Spirit's promptings.

Throughout Jesus' teaching ministry, He frequently used repetition to focus his listener's attention on an important truth. One such statement was *He who has ears to hear, let him hear!* Early in her training Mike determined to develop ears that would correctly hear what God had to say. If He had nothing to say at a certain time, that was alright too.

Mike had simply sold out to Jesus--lock, stock, and barrel!

*****

Jimmy Falso and his wife Tracey were among Mike's favorite people attending *the Abiding Church*. Aside from being Italian, Jimmy was a comedic character with a cheerful countenance and a quick New York wit. He was also a captain in the New York City Police Department, a rank he earned every step of the way from pounding a beat, to detective, and on up the food chain. From his earliest days as a cop in Bedford-Stuyvesant's infamous 41st Precinct, otherwise known as *Fort Apache*, Jimmy discovered that God answered prayers.

He also discovered that the spiritual gifts could rescue him from dangerous situations. One night during a weekly prayer meeting, church members were enjoying a quiet peace in God's presence. Suddenly, Mike clearly saw Jimmy and a partner sitting in a patrol car. However, not more than a hundred feet behind them was an approaching gang of twenty-five to thirty members stretched across the narrow city street.

Immediately Mike spoke up,

Pastor Kyle we need to pray right now for Jimmy Falso and his partner. They are in danger from a street gang.

Quickly nodding his ascent, the group broke into fervent prayer asking God for a wall of protection around Jimmy and his partner. Their prayers were intense, full of urgency, and shorter than anyone expected. The burden had lifted quickly but everyone felt certain that God had intervened in a miraculous way.

And He had!

During that Sunday's church service Jimmy Falso stretched up a hand to share a testimony. He began sharing how he and his partner had been in their parked patrol car in a particularly bad section of the Bronx. Without warning a street full of gang members swarmed around their car but acted as if no one was there. Before Jimmy could utter another word a wave of shouting and praises erupted across the congregation! And then a lady who had attended the prayer meeting stood up and said,

We know Jimmy, believe me we know! Mike saw you sitting there in your patrol car! The Lord rescued you.

The place went wild, Jimmy was safe, and God was praised. It was quite a Sunday!

Chapter 47

Summer 2017, Garden City, New York

Mike had deep affection for both of her in-laws but she couldn't help feeling especially fond of Jack. Gwen was a kindhearted Martha-like figure who was always busy, doing something for others and who simply refused to relax in the normal sense of the word. Whenever Mike and the kids would stop by, her serving clarion would go off and she would disappear into the kitchen to shortly return with hordes of food and goodies.

Jackson and Grace, how about a nice BLT or tuna melt? I also have hamburgers I can cook up or we could get Jack to grill them outside on the patio. Yes, that would be a good idea, we'll get Jack to get things going on the grill.

Jack's call to grilling duties would usually be accompanied by a shrug of his shoulders and a carefully veiled roll of his eyes.

But all grillers should know that Martha-types do not appreciate eyes rolling of any kind!

Jack on the other hand reminded her so much of Mac--easy going, level-headed and full of laughter. You wouldn't think a man who had spent much of his adult life as an NCIS agent and who was now working for the DHS could be so laid back and positive. Mike was not certain about what Jack did at the Department, and the first few times she tried to pry some information out of him he would point his hand towards her like a gun and say,

I'm sorry Mike but if I tell you what I do I'll have to shoot you!

He would immediately start laughing and then reach over to give her a big hug. Mike got the message and stopped asking a lot of questions. However, she recognized that whatever he did had to be very important.

Aside from his pleasant disposition, Mike also knew Jack O'Brien had a deep and abiding faith in Jesus Christ. Early in his naval career as a Master of Arms, Jack had a radical life-altering encounter with Jesus Christ. From that time, he never looked back and together with Gwen they conducted their business and raised their children as a Christian family.

Later as an NCIS field agent, Jack discovered that God's love was also strong and able to miraculously protect those who trusted in Him. On many occasions, Jack would testify in church about escaping a bullet or an assailant's knife. In his line of work, the unexpected was a constant threat but he prayed every day and asked God to send a few angels his way. Mike was certain that Jack's angels never lacked for excitement.

Today Jack did not seem like his normal self so Mike followed him outside to the patio.

Hey Jack, what's going on? You seem to be preoccupied. Anything you want to share and maybe pray about?

Opening the lid on his infrared gas burning grill, he replied,

You could always pick up the clues Mike. Maybe that comes with your prophetic gifting.

I'm just very concerned about the direction our country has been heading in as well as the serious security threats we face. You know I cannot go into details with you about that but I can tell you that we need God's hand of protection. Having such a porous southern border for years hasn't helped either.

Flashing a brief smile Mike answered.

Jack, I want to stay breathing so please, no sharing of deep dark national secrets today! However, I agree with you that our nation is being pulled apart by factions on both sides of the political aisle. The national media is not helping either and I've just about given up trying to find fair and balanced reporting.

But maybe despite everything that is taking place God is moving or is moving certain people into place. I've been reading about the Old Testament prophets and seers who always seemed to show up when things were bad or the Lord wanted a change. On many occasions the sovereignty of God arranged to have those prophetic voices heard by the kings and rulers of their day.

Maybe, God will have a prophetic individual come on the scene whenever he or she is most needed.

Turning away from the grill Jack walked over to his daughter-in-law and wrapped his arm around her shoulder.

Thanks Mike for the encouragement. I know you're right. The earth is the Lord's and that includes everyone on it. He does not surrender His sovereignty to neither man nor devils.

Somehow, He will lead us out of our troubles.

Chapter 48

Then if My people who are called by My name will humble themselves
and pray and seek My face and turn from their wicked ways, I will hear
from heaven and will forgive their sins and restore their land.

2 Chronicles 7:14

26 Sept 2017 the Abiding Church, Garden City,

Pastor Kyle just got off the phone with a friend and church leader in a similar sized congregation in Northern California. He reported that their weekly prayer meeting--usually the least attended activity in the church, had suddenly become the place to be. Members of the church who had never darkened the doors of a prayer service were suddenly showing up with an excitement that was hard to believe. Perhaps even more amazing, young people started showing up and taking their seats right next to the adults.

Kyle, if you were to tell me that my people would become a united praying congregation, I would have respectfully thought you were exercising a faith muscle that you did not possess! But it's happening and all I can say is that I had no part in it whatsoever. It's as if the Holy Spirit shoved me aside and has called these meetings Himself.

Kyle put down the phone and sat quietly thinking for several minutes. That wasn't the first time he caught wind of something usual happening in both large and smaller churches across the land. As part of a loose knit prophetic association of over two hundred congregations, similar stories kept cropping up on the East Coast, the *fly-over states,* and even in the heart of liberal strongholds on the West Coast.

Although no longer traveling a lot, Kyle kept running across further evidence that God was on the move. Twenty-four hours prayer centers and special prayer vigils involving people from all denominations were becoming far more common. He also knew that in several Gospel passages, Jesus quoted a prophetic word given to Isaiah that *My Temple will be called a House of Prayer for all nations.* From his studies of church history, every move of the Holy Spirit beginning with the Day of Pentecost had been characterized by a praying people whose petitions literally paved the way for heaven to touch earth.

Something was stirring deep within Pastor Kyle's heart and he quietly slipped out of his chair and slid down to his knees.

Dear God in heaven I believe that You are moving throughout the land and You are placing a passion to pray in Your people's hearts. Please don't leave us out Lord. Grant us grace to become a House of Prayer right here in Garden City.

I'll step out of the way Lord. I promise. You can have all the glory and honor.

As the man of God continued to plead his case, an intense desperation rose up within him until his words became tears and his tears liquid words!

And that pleased the Lord!

*****

The next few church prayer meetings seemed like a contradiction of terms. The summer months were taking their toll and only a handful of people would show up. Most of these individuals seemed to be filling an obligation rather than expecting an encounter of the God-kind. It was disheartening and though Kyle was tempted to let the burden go, a small glowing ember still flickered inside.

On the last Sunday of September, his announcement regarding the Tuesday evening prayer service was met with the same indifference it usually received. *Oh well,* he thought, *God, I'm going to show up even if no one else does.*

On the way to church that Tuesday night, Kyle and his wife had an animated conversation about great moves of God to include the celebrated Hebrides Revival of 1949. Two elderly sisters--one blind and the other filled with arthritis, prayed from ten in the evening until three in the morning, twice a week for years! But one day, God showed up and His Presence moved across the wind-swept islands of the Hebrides chain. Of special note, most of the people touched by God were not in a church building or service.

The Lord simply found them wherever they were!

Pulling up in the parking lot, neither Kyle nor Diane knew what to expect but something was going on in their hearts. They opened the church and set up the normal number of chairs and then sat down to wait on whoever would show up that night.

And the first Person to show up was the Spirit of God!

By the time the first church member arrived, Kyle and Diane were prostrate on the floor with hot tears running down their cheeks. Within seconds, that individual had joined them on the carpet as well. Then a couple showed up with the same results. Some folks never got past the foyer as the Holy Spirit continued leading His kind of a prayer meeting.

Surprisingly, a van full of believers nobody knew pulled into the parking lot while returning from one of their denomination's retreat. Intending to ask about using the church's restrooms, two people went into the building but didn't return. Others in the van began to get irritated and so they set off together to retrieve the delinquents.

As they stepped through the front doors, they saw their two friends lying in a heap and wailing like nobody they had ever seen before. And before you know it, there was another heap of believers who had entered God's House of Prayer.

*****

In the weeks following the Holy Spirit's invasion, God continued to clean up and knit hearts with a love that no longer saw distinctions or denominational differences. It was family time in the Kingdom and once that had been achieved the Spirit switched gears.

And those gears had to do with the nation. It was time for people to seek the Lord and turn from their wickedness that He might hear from heaven, forgive sins, and heal the land.

It was time!

Chapter 49

Located approximately sixty-two miles from the hustle-bustle and stress of the nation's capital, Camp David is the President of the United States' official private retreat. Set among the wooden hills of Catoctin Mountain Park it has been used by every president beginning with FDR and it was a favorite of President Ronald Reagan who once hosted Prime Minister Margaret Thatcher there.

After a first visit, President Rizzo thought it too rustic and would have preferred his own palatial resort in Florida. Nevertheless, it was much easier to conduct the business at hand with cabinet members in the nearby Maryland woods. The topic of discussion would be Iran, a thorn in the side of every U.S. administration since the Shah's ouster in 1979.

Meeting in the Laurel Lodge conference room, the president provided an introduction.

Thank you all for coming and I hope the staff has you all comfortably taken care of. If you need anything, you know the drill.

Smiling he continued, *Ask and it shall be given to you.*

Now before we start the meeting, I invited the Chaplain of the Senate, a man you all know, to lead us in prayer as we surely need the wisdom of heaven.

Nodding to the retired Navy Rear Admiral, the president took his seat at the head of the conference table. The former Chief of Navy Chaplains closed his eyes and searched his soul. Shortly later he began,

God in heaven, we are gathered here to decide on matters of great importance that will not only affect this nation but many nations. We are not sufficient in our own wisdom to do so nor are our agendas always right in Your sight.

Please forgive us for our assumptions, our mistakes which inadvertently have caused harm, and for the sins of the land, which are too many to recount. We are a people who have strayed but we ask for Your mercy and wisdom tonight.

Please heal our land and restore us as a people who know their God.

And without another word, the Chaplain picked up his bible and walked directly out the set of double doors.

Then glancing at each face in the room, the president broke the silence.

I really like that man and I think God really likes him also. And make no mistake we needed that prayer tonight as we find a way to undo the horrific nuclear deal with Iran I have been left with.

*****

In July of 2015, a Joint Comprehensive Plan of Action was agreed to between Iran and the five permanent members of the UN Security Council plus Germany. The group, otherwise known as P5+1, sought to reduce the number of Iranian centrifuges from 19,000 to 6,104, reduce stockpiles of enriched uranium, and allow for inspections of all its nuclear facilities, supply chains, and uranium mining sites.

The agreement was a contentious political issue in the U.S. as it was never submitted to Congress for ratification because it had no chance of passing. In effect the former president ran an end-around play forcing the American public to live with terms of an agreement that well…never went public.

But what's a small thing like that when presidents want to further their legacies?

Tehran on the other hand, pocketed one hundred billion dollars in sanction relief and had a deal that merely delayed but did not stop the regime from achieving a breakout nuclear capability. Considering Iran's compliance track record and support for terrorist organizations, President Rizzo thought the agreement not only a bad deal but one that would sooner, rather than later, threaten the sovereignty of Israel.

Now with Hezbollah's recent attacks, Rizzo wanted to send the mullahs a message…no, a series of messages they would not forget.

*****

The SECSTATE took the floor.

Mr. President, I have several suggestions in the form of reprisals against the Iranians.

First, I suggest we pull completely out of the accord which will not require any haggling with Congress since they never had the opportunity to sign off on it. None of the other P5+1 reps will scream much since their governments hadn't signed off on it either.

Next, we should dust off every sanction and reapply them with a vengeance until the Iranians completely muzzle Hezbollah.

In wrapping this up, I wouldn't spend much time pursuing additional sanctions through the UN, and with a smile, he added, *especially since it remains on your most unfavorable organization list!*

Happy with the Secretary's recommendations, the president then looked around the room,

Are there other suggestions we should consider?

The Secretary of Defense raised his hand and cleared his throat.

Sir, I believe there are several other measures we can kick around. Israel's Iron Dome system has a good batting average but they've been swatting at swarms of flies. We should offer them our latest aerial defense batteries to help them get back on their feet.

Next, and at least for the next six to eight months, we should send to the region additional Naval warships equipped with the Aegis ballistic missile defense systems.

And although this is more in the SECSTATE's department, I suggest sir that when hostilities clear up over there, you pay the Prime Minister of Israel a visit. It will do wonders for their morale and it will send a clear message to the Iranians.

The group worked for another hour and then without further discussion, the President stood up and thanked everyone for their contributions. He then offered his final comments.

I understand with this current Iranian regime, we're dealing with an unpredictable and highly dangerous enemy. Remember, in their eyes we're the Great Satan.

I was elected to protect the American people and I am not interested in further entanglements in the Middle East. But I learned from my dad that bullies have a short shelf life when they are faced with strength.

I intend to display strength to an Iranian government who has assumed that we are a weak and an uncommitted people.

We are not and they will shortly discover that truth for themselves.

As he finished speaking, the attendees stood as the forty-fifth president of the United States exited the conference room.

Chapter 50

1 October 2017, Oceanside, New York

I t was little more than a month into a new school year. As high school students, both had become increasingly more independent, a reality that often bucked against Mike's black and white view of the world. The real clashing of wills usually took place between mother and daughter with Jackson wise enough to maintain his status as a neutral party.

As his father used to do, whenever hostilities threatened the domestic peace, Jackson would boldly state that he was leaving the house to join the Peace Corp. And then with exaggerated gestures he would march to the front door shouting out, *let's give peace a chance!* That would usually break the ice and calm the raging seas.

But on this Sunday afternoon all was peaceful in their Cape Cod house. The church service that morning was awesome and Mike took part in a prophetic presbytery that included her pastors as well as a visiting minister from Northern Ireland. The ministry brought prophetic insights and encouragement to many in the church and Mike just loved being a part of it. Everything spoken during the presbytery was public and judged by the leadership. On numerous occasions Mike had witnessed the power of a word from God to literally transform a person's life.

And now she would soon have the house to herself. Jackson agreed to drive his sister to Roosevelt Field Mall, the tenth largest mall in the country, where they would shop and then take in a movie with friends. That was fine with Mike as she decided to read a little and spend time outside on the patio beside her in-ground pool.

It was a gorgeous day, several notches above the monthly average of 65 degrees Fahrenheit, and without a cloud in the sky. Again, Mike's thoughts turned to the morning's events.

Thank You God for giving me opportunity to use Your gifts to bless others. It's such a joy when light replaces darkness and hope is revived and dreams are launched. And thank You for my children and please keep them safe tonight.

She then laid back in her chaise lounge, closed her eyes and soaked in the warm sun rays. Within minutes Mike curled her body to one side and drifted off into a deep but disturbed sleep.

*****

Somewhere in her dream state, Mike discovered herself looking down from a concrete platform at a very long and sleek submarine sitting in an underground sub pen. Although it did not have U.S. Navy markings she distinctly remembered thinking that it was huge and like the Ohio class of subs that Mac had taken her to see during a visit to Kings Point, Georgia.

Several sailors accompanied by four heavily armed guards, loaded two metal containers on deck and then as she continued watching they lowered their cargo into the hull of the sub. The containers were handled with extreme care and the guards went below deck with the cargo. As she continued looking at the sub, she remembered shuddering with an intense sense of foreboding.

A moment later, she found herself walking through a narrow gangway and following the sailors and guards she had seen above deck. They brought the containers to a room with caged enclosure which they then locked and secured. A yellow and black sign hung near the cage. Out in the gangway, a grim-faced guard then took a position outside the door.

In a final scene, she watched the sub leave its pen and head out to open waters on a very important mission. Again, she couldn't shake the thought that the sub and its strange cargo was somehow menacing. In fact, she remembered feeling very, very frightened and then she woke up!

*****

Since it was the church's prayer night, Mike served up a quick risotto and chicken dinner for the family. Jack and Diane were on their way over and she would go on to the meeting with her father-in-law while Diane stayed to help Jackson and Grace with their math. The subject had never been Mike's strong suit and she was thankful her mother-in-law had taught virtually every math course offered in public high schools.

Plus, the kids always enjoyed Gwen who would probably end up baking *a little something* while she was there.

As for Mike she couldn't shake the sense of foreboding she had sensed in her dream the day before. She thought to herself,

I need to get this thing off me tonight. There's nothing like a good prayer meeting to set things straight again.

Hearing the doorbell, she let in her in-laws, issued her kids their marching orders, and gave Gwen a big hug for helping Jackson and Grace with their math. Then turning to Jack, she said,

I'm ready Jack and I can't wait to get to the meeting tonight. If we leave now we'll be able to get a decent seat. It's been incredible seeing how hungry and committed so many people have become.

Opening the front door, Jack yelled out to his wife who was already setting up camp at the kitchen table,

We'll bring back the glory Gwen, and with a little chuckle he added, *and we'll try to be back before midnight!*

*****

The meeting was powerful and it got off the ground right away when Pastor Kyle began praying for the nation. In a sovereign work of the Spirit, most, if not all of those in attendance had their prayer lives flipped right side up. Gone were the self-centeredness, the half-hearted petitions, and uncertainties whether God really heard their prayers or not. The prophet Daniel penned the following words while in Babylonian captivity.

...the people who know their God shall be strong, and carry out great exploits.

That night the people of God were strong and great exploits had been accomplished through faith and tears. In a divine contradiction, the Lord determined that weak things would shame those things considered mighty. Looking around at huddled groups of individuals praying on their knees it would have been quite easy to minimize what was taking place.

Mike loved the profound wisdom of God in choosing the disciplines of faith and prayer to move mountains on earth.

*****

Driving back from the church, Jack sat with an unusually quiet daughter-in-law. Wanting to probe the silence he cheerfully commented on the gathering.

Great meeting tonight Mike!

However, he did not get much of a response as Mike simply agreed with him.

Yes, it was.

More silence followed. Jack decided to cut to the chase and asked,

Mike is anything wrong? We just had a tremendous meeting and everybody there sensed the presence of God and if I'm not mistaken, you seem as if you're carrying a heavy weight.

Jack wheeled his old Honda Accord with a gazillion miles on it into Mike's driveway, shut the motor off, and turned in his seat to face her.

What's going on Mike?

Measuring her words, she answered,

Yesterday while sitting beside the pool I fell asleep and had a terrifying dream. It's been with me all day and I had hoped it would lift during the prayer meeting.

Jack, I realize that many dreams are inspired by late night raids to the kitchen or events or anxieties picked up during the day. Then on occasion God breaks into our sleeping moments and we are given something that He wants to reveal or warn us about. The meanings are often difficult to understand and may require that we pray and dig into the Scriptures for understanding.

When the dream foreshadows an urgent event as was the case with the infant Jesus, angels gave Joseph precise instructions to flee to Egypt and escape Herod.

Pausing a moment, Mike stared at her hands and continued.

Jack, what I'm about to tell you seemed so real and so very evil that I remembered shaking in my dream.

And for the next thirty minutes Mike shared every detail of her dream with her father-in-law.

Chapter 51

3 October 2017, Garden City

With a cappuccino in each hand, Gwen sat down opposite her husband at the little table beside their kitchen. Sliding the steaming cup of Italian go-juice to Jack she smiled and joked,

Tomorrow, it's your turn to make the cappuccinos. Today it's on me but I'm giving you fair warning, I'll be off-duty when the sun rises in the morning!

Without a trace of his characteristic cheer, Jack merely nodded while muttering a weak, *thanks Gwen.* After several uncomfortable minutes, Gwen couldn't take it any longer and she put the brakes on a *going-nowhere* breakfast.

Jack O'Brien, look at me! I'm right here! Remember I'm you wife and I am quite certain that before I sat down you were still my husband!

What's going on with you?

Gwen's words hit the mark and Jack shook off his deep thoughts to offer a quick apology.

Hey, I'm sorry Gwen. I didn't mean to shut you out this morning and with a wink he added, *especially since you served the king his cappuccino the way he likes it!*

Feigning offense Gwen responded,

Oh, so you're a king are you! Let me inform your majesty that I am queen of this kitchen and you are merely a guest at my table!

Chuckling Jack yielded.

I stand--or sit, very much corrected, your highness.

Okay now that we've settled matters of state, what's going on Jack? Why the pensiveness?

Before answering, Jack took a long sip of his coffee and then leaned towards his wife.

It's something that Mike shared with me last night.

You mean when you were both in the car and sitting in the driveway?

Yes, and I certainly hadn't planned on keeping you waiting for nearly an hour, but that's when she decided to download a recent dream.

Growing more curious Gwen stated,

I'm assuming you both thought it was a God-dream?

Well I wasn't too sure at the beginning but by the time Mike finished I was convinced. The dream was detailed and it involved her observing two containers being loaded on a large submarine and then placed in a secure area with a strange placard attached to it. As she described the submarine I realized that it had to be a boomer--you know, a sub large enough to launch ballistic missiles.

It reminded her of a U.S. Ohio-class sub that she had seen with Mac years ago at Kings Point.

In a more serious tone, Jack added,

There were two more disturbing facts. First, Mike was certain that it was not a U.S. sub and secondly, the entire panorama left her with an overwhelming sense of foreboding.

With a concerned look on her face Gwen asked,

Jack, was she able to see the crew or the men with the containers?

Yes Gwen, she did…and the crew was Asian and quite possibly Chinese or North Korean!

Goodness Jack, that can't be good. Do we need to start praying about this and ask the Lord for His wisdom?

That's what I was sorting through earlier Gwen. I kept thinking about that terrorist cell we at Homeland Security, along with the FBI and local officials, had busted out in Suffolk County about two years ago. Thankfully it didn't receive much press coverage and if you recall, we nabbed three Muslim men from Somalia and a woman who had downloaded a cook book for making improvised bombs. They had set up a makeshift lab and by the time we raided the place, they had put the finishing touches on two IEDs.

Gwen thought for a moment and then her face lit up.

I remember that Jack and I also recall Mike having had a vision during a worship service in which she clearly saw a street sign, house numbers and then she heard the word, terror.

Jack replied, *you are categorically correct Gwen.*

Although it was a tough sell to my superiors that our daughter-in-law could have seen the location of some bad people intent on harming innocent Americans, it was a call from Jimmy Falso which helped to tip the scales.

But after we had the group in custody no one questioned what Mike had seen. Not a single person involved in the case!

Getting up from the table, Gwen walked over to her husband and gave him a brief hug.

Okay Jack O'Brien, now what? What are we to do with this?

Jack quickly replied,

We'll do what we know to do Gwen. We'll pray and as always, God has answers even before we even ask the first question! I'll also call the pastors and see if we can't discreetly begin lifting this up during the weekly prayer meeting.

Finishing the conversation Jack added,

It's possible that Mike's dream is less threatening than it appears. Also, we can easily mix up the literal and the spiritual meaning as well. Ultimately, if the dream contains a warning from God, He'll have to provide the understanding.

Okay, Gwen I'm off to work. I'll be home late this evening so don't bother cooking anything for me. I'll pick up my usual Reuben sandwich from the deli.

And with a quick kiss to his wife's cheek, Jack left the house to help defend the lives of his fellow Americans.

Chapter 52

5 October 2017, Undisclosed Location, Iran

U tter rage was too tame a phrase to describe the reaction of Iran's leader's to the news of their dissolved nuclear agreement and reapplied sanctions. To their dismay though their wrath was largely wasted on a president whose administration was not willing to make any concessions whatsoever! Instead the mullahs faced a U.S. leadership team more resembling a screaming eagle with the Gadsden flag's famous *don't tread on me* words written across its chest.

In addition, things in Lebanon were going badly for their Hezbollah surrogates despite the fact well over a million Israeli's had either fled the northern border or were holed up in bomb shelters. The Iron Dome system had worked better than advertised but defense batteries could not entirely handle the sheer volume of missiles raining down on Jewish cities. Casualties were reported in Haifa, Nahariyya, Nazareth and dozens of smaller towns even as far south as Netanya and Tel-Aviv.

Each hour sirens would wail, drowning out the screams of the yet untreated wounded, victims of the last ground-shaking attack delivered by Iranian-built missiles. But like a wounded animal, Israel's air and ground forces were exacting a terrific toll on their enemies.

In a remarkable, but previously thought impossible, amphibious landing, the IDF landed over 25,000 soldiers and their armored elements near Byblos, considered the oldest port in the world. The invasion force then linked up with two brigades of the 98th Paratrooper's Division in a combined-arms drive that effectively cut the nation in two. Hezbollah forces found themselves trapped between an anvil and the hammering assaults launched at them from across the Israel border.

It would be a matter of days before the IDF choked the life out of the encircled Iranian-backed forces.

*****

The Supreme Leader, surrounded by the heads of Iran's Ministry of Intelligence & Security [MOIS], the Islamic Revolutionary Guard Corp [IRGC], the regular army, and the Supreme National Security Council, was in a particularly foul mood.

We have bled the Jews but now we must teach this American president a lesson he will never forget. We do not yet have the nuclear capacity to challenge the U.S. but our ways have always been the way of stealth and intrigue. The Americans do not have the stomach for mass casualties much less the strength and courage that comes from fighting a just and holy cause.

Yet we must strike them with the skill and violence of The Hashshashin, Persia's legionary Shia Assassins, who struck fear in the courts of the entire region. We must thrust a dagger into America in such a way that will leave no signs to our Republic.

With Allah's help we shall succeed.

Then dismissing the attendees, he asked the heads of the IRGC and MOIS to remain. When the room was clear, he first addressed the IRGC's commander, General Mahmoud Ali.

General Ali how many dirty bombs have we purchased from the North Koreans?

We have paid for six but we have received only two. The Koreans are balking over our non-payment for the guidance systems for our medium range missiles. Our scientists claim they are faulty and the Koreans are unwilling to admit any problems. We are at an impasse.

Then turning to the head of the MOIS, Iran's Ayatollah asked,

If you were to strike an American city to cause as much economical and psychological damage as possible, where would you attack?

That is quite easy to answer my Leader. New York City is their financial and banking center. Moreover, since 9/11 it has become a symbol of their national will and spirit.

A faint smile emerged on the Supreme Leader's otherwise stoic face.

Very good! That is my assessment as well.

Brothers, in the tradition of the Hashshashin, I want you to secretly plunge the assassin's dagger right into the back of America's most prominent city.

Only this time, the weapon of choice will be a very dirty and very lethal nuclear bomb. We will distance ourselves from the current conflict, appear docile and accepting of their demands, and seek Allah for the right time to strike.

The two men nodded in agreement and prepared to leave, when Iran's leader held up a hand.

And one more thing brothers! We will pit our enemies against one another and attribute the attack to those ISIS dogs who are recklessly striking European capitals while threatening the U.S.

Yes, it will be ISIS who will find itself the target of America's wrath! What could be more just!

Chapter 53

2 Kings 6: 18-22

As the Aramean [Syrian] army advanced towards him, Elisha prayed, *O Lord, please make them blind.* So, the Lord struck them with blindness as Elisha had asked.

It shouldn't be considered odd that the God who opens the eyes of a servant to see mountains full of fiery horses and chariots could also close the eyes of an invading army so that they could not recognize the man they were pursuing. But that's exactly what took place outside the city of Dothan that day.

The prophet whose strength and shield were God boldly approached a sightless band of warriors wondering why their lights had been turned off. In response to their inquiries he volunteered his help,

This is not the way, nor is this the city. Follow me, and I will take you to the man you seek.

And so, the man they were seeking led them straight into Samaria, the capital city of the ten northern tribes of Israel. Passing through the city gates, the Syrians found themselves surrounded and at the mercy of their captors. Once again, the prophet prayed and God heard him.

Lord, open the eyes of these men, that they may see.

And what a surprise it must have been! There on every side were heavily armed Israelites eager to send their hated enemies to the realms of their dead gods! Even the king got in the act,

My father, shall I kill them? Shall I kill them?

But the prophet would have none of it. He hadn't invoked the name and power of the Almighty God to slaughter hapless men, who ignorantly found themselves on the wrong side of heaven! Instead Elisha insisted the king provide both food and drink before sending them back to their master unharmed.

*****

Mercy triumphs over judgment.

Miraculous interventions are designed to teach the human heart what it should know about God. One who saw heavenly horses and chariots no longer feared. Blinded warriors serving blind gods realized that Israel's God was powerful but more incredibly, He was merciful.

Each man walked back to Syria knowing that Jehovah was different from all other gods. Their eyes which had been blinded to their natural surroundings were now opened to new spiritual truths.

God's ways are higher than man's and His mercies never cease. They are new every morning and every evening.

Chapter 54

8 October 2017, the Abiding Church, Garden City

I t was Saturday morning and Pastor Kyle sat in his office and quietly meditated on Jesus' words to His disciples in Mark's eleventh chapter:

...whatever things you ask when you pray, believe that you receive them, and you will have them...

Jesus was offering His followers another illustrated sermon on faith while using a dried-up fig tree as a backdrop. Kyle noted that the Lord emphasized the asking and believing side of prayer as opposed to the way many people often told God how to fix things. He knew that the Lord didn't need any help from him in running the universe.

However, in less than thirty minutes members of the church would begin streaming in; some coming and going, and others staying for the entire three-hour block of time dedicated to praying for the nation. Recently, God has moved upon the congregation in a way that freed many people to recognize that prayer was one of the highest forms of communication possible with the God of heaven. The effect had revolutionized the church! Looking up at his clock, he knew it was time to get things started and as he left his desk he whispered,

God please help us to pray and see or hear whatever You want us to.

*****

Mike couldn't get to the meeting until the last hour but she was okay with that and she was certain the Lord was also. As soon as she stepped into the foyer of the church she could sense an amazing presence of God which almost took her breath away. It was as if a thick but invisible cloud had settled on the building. Stepping through the double doors into the sanctuary, she saw about a dozen people, some prostrate on the floor, some on their knees, and others up near the altar silently weeping.

No one said a word and there was very little movement. She entered the room largely unnoticed except for Pastor Kyle who merely nodded at her. Not wanting to disturb anyone, Mike found a chair, sat down, and as she had done on many occasions started quietly thanking God for His presence and blessings.

But she soon found herself in an entirely different setting. Her humanly formed words almost seemed profane--an affront to the royal silence demanded of an awesome and holy Being! The weight of His glory was an irresistible force pressing her body to the carpeted floor. Though Mike was certain of God's love and in turn, she loved Him with every fiber in her body, she was nearly paralyzed with fear. It was not the fear of a startled person or a response generated by some eternal threat. Instead it was the indescribable dread experienced when mortal flesh contacts the Almighty. When God removed the veil of His glory, the prophet Isaiah cried out, *Woe is me, I am undone* and the Apostle John collapsed to the ground as though a dead man.

The fear of the Lord was in the room and everyone there knew it! Within a Hebrew context, the fear of the Lord produced a deep reverence coupled with a certain element of terror! Never had Mike felt so powerless and dependent upon God's rich mercy just to remain alive and breathing.

Mike couldn't tell how long the experience lasted only that at a certain point there was a shift followed by an enveloping love; the second part of the night's Divinity lesson. It was in a lull between successive waves of liquid love that she heard the Lord.

Daughter, I'm allowing you to hear plans intended to harm your nation. Pay close attention to what you hear and do not be afraid to tell others the words that have been spoken.

And then she listened to the ranting plot of a mad man.

We will repay the Americans in a way they will never forget. As they sought to take my life, now many will suffer the consequences.

Their president has tried to bully me and strangle the lifeblood of this glorious country. His forces have surrounded us and he has constantly plotted against us with those South Korean dogs. He sent his lackeys to my capital city to do me harm. And now…Yes now, I will strike back at the city where he made his billions.

Yes, I will indeed strike New York City--the very apple of his eye!

*****

Afterwards, Mike grabbed her Apple phone and with trembling fingers she typed every word into her Notes app. She felt overwhelmed and completely drained by the night's events. After making her way out to the church parking lot, she looked towards the night sky and asked,

Why me Lord? Why me?

Not expecting--or even wanting an answer, she got into her car and drove home. Tomorrow she would figure out what to do but tonight, she was going to bed and sleep for as long as it was humanly possible.

Chapter 55

The day after...2017, Garden City

Mike woke up after nine a.m.--a first for her in many years. Apparently, the kids had gotten themselves off to school as Jackson's car was no longer parked in the driveway. The best guess was that brother and sister were civil enough to handle breakfast without mom's supervision and then, just like independent, level-headed high school students they headed out for a cheery day of learning.

As she turned on her Nespresso coffee machine, she tried a happy thought of the day.

I bet Jackson and Grace come home this afternoon full of knowledge and conventional wisdom--and without math homework!

Her mind then meandered back to the previous night's events at the church. An extra strong number twelve coffee pod selection was helpful and the ensuing caffeine surge swept away the remaining nocturnal cobwebs. Reaching for her phone, she opened the Notes app and re-read the words of a man whose hatred for the United States and her president could almost be felt. The venom-filled content was exactly as she remembered it and she shuddered a bit over the possible implications.

Weighed down with a burden she couldn't deal with, much less understand, Mike turned her heart to heaven.

Oh Lord God what do I do with all this--the dream and now these incredibly threatening words from a man I've never seen or met. I do not doubt that You have given me the ability to see and hear things not possible in the natural realm. But now what do I do and who do I talk to?

I don't mind telling You that I feel way in over my head. Please grant me the strength, courage and wisdom that I need. Thank You!

After praying, she sat quietly and expectantly before the Lord, a spiritual discipline honed over many years of practice. Not long after, she picked up her mobile phone and dialed the first of two numbers.

God's response had been enough to get her to first base--but Mike would have to run the remaining bases to home plate!

*****

The small group sat comfortably in the Hanson's family room. In attendance were the pastors, the O'Brien's, the Falso's and of course, Mike. Her first phone call had been to Pastor Kyle and the second, to her father-in-law. It was Jack who suggested that Jimmy and Tracey also join the meeting and Mike was very happy to see them both.

After the coffees and teas had been distributed, Pastor Kyle looked around the room and said,

Before we get started tonight I am convinced that what the Lord has allowed Mike to experience is the real deal. It is not an understatement to say that critical spiritual battles are being fought in heavenly realms with repercussions felt on earth.

The destinies of nations and people are at stake and God has always used men and women to hear what He wanted them to hear and to see what human eyes could never see.

Now as we join in prayer, let us ask God for His favor, wisdom and strength to thwart every wicked plan against our land. We need His strategy and it's critical we know our next step.

And their fervent prayers lasted well into the night.

Chapter 56

16 October 2017, New York City

Officially, the Callahan's drive down to Manhattan was to evaluate the possible acquisition of a cash-strapped competitor. Then of course Jin Lee would have to pay a visit to Sachs Fifth Avenue and several other favorite New York City shops to show her support for local merchants. However, the unofficial but primary reason for the trip was to determine how best to cripple the Big Apple.

Forgoing their usual chauffeured ride throughout the city, *Jimbo* drove their new 2017 Mercedes GLS 63 SUV with its 577-horsepower engine and all the bells and whistles that came with a Premium 1 Package. They both agreed that a drive through the Thanksgiving Day Parade's actual route would help in determining the most lethal locations for their *little surprises*. Then with plenty of time on their hands they conducted their own farewell tour, going to the Lower East

Side, Little Italy, the Financial District, then Midtown's Soho and Chelsea areas, and finally, Uptown with its parks and world-famous museums. Driving through so many familiar sights and with their accompanying memories, *Jimbo* had a fleeting moment of nostalgia.

Oh well, he thought, *a job is a job and if Manhattan must go, so be it!*

*****

Unlike a dirty bomb or a Radiological Dispersal Device which used a conventional explosive such as dynamite to spread radioactive waste over an area, each backpack had a five-kiloton yield.

The projected damage zone for such a bomb was horrific: Few, if any, buildings would be left standing within a mile radius of the detonation and with virtually no survivors. For several miles outside the blast radius there would be substantial structural damage to buildings, utility lines, automobiles, with caved-in roofs, and fires. Injuries from blown out glass and debris would be extensive as well as exposure to elevated radioactivity levels.

Manhattan was one of the most densely populated areas on the planet with over 1.6 million people living in a land area of 22.83 square miles or 71,900 residents per square mile. On normal business days...and especially on parade days, Manhattan's numbers would climb closer to 4 million unsuspecting souls.

The island's geography worked against its survivability. The length of Manhattan from Battery Park to the Henry Hudson bridge was only 13.11 miles. Two well placed bombs would leave the borough in ruin, its lingering radioactive halo hampering efforts to recover the injured as well as later efforts to rebuild.

If successfully carried out, the assault on Manhattan would be one of the deadliest attacks the world has ever seen.

Chapter 57

17 October 2017, Presidential Bedroom Suite

President Rizzo tossed and turned for the better part of an hour before giving up on the notion of sleep. A notorious late night and early rising workaholic, America's chief executive was grudgingly forced to admit that corporate pressures paled in the face of presidential duties and responsibilities. Now staring into the darkness of the Presidential Bedroom Suite, he decided to head to the Family Kitchen located at the northwest corner of the White House's Second Floor.

He eased out of the bed, careful to avoid disturbing the First Lady, and slipped out the door. He had a short walk across the West Sitting Hall before entering the kitchen previously redesigned by Jackie Kennedy during the family's abbreviated stay in the White House.

The president was alone and that was exactly what he had hoped for. Opening the refrigerator, he searched around until he found the prize--two cannoli's strategically hidden behind a loaf of bread. Then he made himself an espresso--for how could anyone eat cannoli without a bit of coffee?

After polishing off the Italian delights, he tried to empty his mind from the thousand and one concerns that came with the job. But lately there was something else and he couldn't quite put his finger on it. Yet, it lingered and at times he felt a fear, as if someone or something was trying to wrap its fingers around his throat.

The president had not been a particularly religious man although he knew enough of the forms and traditions. Yet during his candidacy, he received strong support from many Christian leaders representing a variety of faiths and denominations. Later, he had the pleasure of meeting praying men and women who expressed a genuine concern for him, his family, and for the welfare of the nation.

These people were not selling anything or trying to get presidential fingers to leverage personal ambitions. Truthfully, Rizzo felt quite comfortable with them and he especially welcomed the peace and joy they brought to the table. A much smaller group of believers had surprised him with remarkably accurate prophetic messages concerning his election and presidency. Their words were generally encouraging but there was also warning.

Maybe his recent feelings and the prophetic warnings were connected? He didn't know but since he was up in the middle of the night, the president thought he might try praying himself.

And so, he did.

God, you understand that I don't know you very well. And if it's true that You had a hand in my becoming president I want to personally thank You.

I can see that the job is much bigger and far more demanding that I ever thought it would be and I would really appreciate Your help.

And God, I don't know if I'm doing this right or not but would You please protect this land and the people that I love. I believe You love them too God.

Thanks for listening. I'm going to go back to bed now.

It's interesting how God draws men and women to Himself.

Chapter 58

The Department of Homeland Security or DHS, was established in the wake of the 9/11 attack in 2001 and with over 240,000 employees, it was the third largest cabinet department. Formed from 22 different federal agencies into a single unified organization, the DHS was chartered to develop a national strategy to protect the homeland and safeguard its citizens from future terrorist attacks. As part of its overall mission, the department also managed the country's borders, administered immigration laws, secured cyberspace, and strengthened national disaster responses.

In a sense, it was an anti-terrorism one-stop-shop with a lot of side bar activity attached.

Due to his NCIS experience, Jack was an ideal fit as a DHS antiterrorist expert. On any given day he could find himself involved with aviation security, cargo screening, dealing with international partners, and providing support to state, local, and even tribal law enforcement agencies.

As a national security agency, over ninety percent of DHS employees were stationed outside of the Washington D.C. which helped Jack land a job in the New York City area. The work however was a continuing challenge. Despite years of experience as a law enforcement professional, the sheer volume and complexity of potential threats could simply stagger a person. There were chemical, biological, radiological, nuclear, and cyber threats which were constantly evolving and could come from abroad or from homegrown sources.

That's why Jack prayed every day for God's help in protecting the nation and enabling him to perform his job.

*****

Jack's immediate supervisor ran the NYC field office and in his humble opinion, the man was utterly unsuited for the job with little law enforcement or counter-terrorism experience. Yet after the prayer meeting the night before, everyone agreed that Jack should address Mike's dream and the words given to her with his boss first. Despite his initial misgivings, Jack decided to salute smartly and see what happened.

Stan Hanover was at his desk and dressed in an expensive three-piece suit and three hundred-dollar shoes that rarely left the office. Knocking on Stan's open door, Jack entered the room, sat in a chair, and angled it so he could directly face him.

Stan, I want to share with you what I believe is a significant and credible threat to our country and uniquely to this city.

The seriousness of his best agent's tone caused Stan Hanover to stop figuring out his monthly credit card expenses and to focus on what he was hearing.

What do you mean Jack? What kind of threat are we talking about and who or what are your credible sources?

Without a pause Agent O'Brien answered,

The threat may be some version of a dirty bomb or even a backpack or suitcase nuke intended for New York City. My source is my daughter-in-law Mike.

With an incredulous look, Stan responded,

Your daughter-in-law is a credible source for a possible major attack on the nation's most important city? Come on Jack, what are you thinking? Is this an early build-up to April's Fools Day?

Expecting resistance Jack continued.

Stan, I realize what this sounds like on your end but just hear me out for a few minutes. Almost two years ago, and before you arrived here in the office, we worked with the FBI and local law enforcement in Suffolk County to take down a budding Somali terrorist cell. The reason we succeeded was because my daughter-in-law had a vision during a church service and she clearly saw a street sign, house numbers and then she heard the word, terror.

Your predecessor thought it was crazy too but we were getting chatter about a possible bombing and we had absolutely no leads.

Jack continued,

We broke the cell up as they were putting the finishing touches on a few improvised weapons and it was Mike's information that enabled us to get the job done.

Recently she had a dream and an experience in which she heard the words of someone identifying New York City as a target.

Before he could continue, Jack was interrupted with a well-practiced stony look.

Listen Jack, I'm not a religious man--never have been, and I can't explain what happened two years ago. Maybe there was an atmospheric disturbance or something less dramatic.

But if you think I'm going to go out on a huge limb because your daughter-in-law saw and heard something and I don't mind adding, without corroborating support, you're crazy!

Trying to remain calm despite a team of angry horses straining at the bit, Jack answered.

Look Stan I'm not a rookie. In Mike's vision, she described either a Chinese or North Korean submarine being loaded with two small and tightly secured containers. The containers were stowed in the sub inside an enclosure which had what I believed was a radioactive placard.

The words she heard cited an American assassination attempt on some leader who in turn, was vowing to make this country pay by attacking New York. The only leader I know who could possibly have felt that way is the guy in North Korea.

It's circumstantial, I know but it makes sense!

Stan Hanover was not convinced and in ending the discussion he added,

Sorry Jack. It may make sense to you but not to me. I'm not going anywhere with it.

Now get out of my office.

Quickly leaving the room, Jack tried to keep his emotions in check as he grabbed his jacket to take a walk. Once outside the building, he paused on the sidewalk and before walking off he murmured a quick prayer.

Lord, that didn't go well did it? I guess this is Strike One for the home team.

Please God! You must help us or something terrible is going to happen to this city.

But God already had a plan and He was sticking to it…

Chapter 59

18 October 2017, 1 Police Plaza, Manhattan, NYC

J ack kept walking until he arrived at his favorite Starbucks where he paid for an emergency double espresso. Sitting outside under an umbrella topped table, he speed-dialed Jimmy Falso with an update of his meeting.

Hey Jimmy, this is Jack. Can you talk?

Minutes before the call, Captain Jimmy Falso had threatened his people in the NYPD's Intelligence Bureau with a painful and unusual death if any of them dared to interrupt him for next sixty minutes.

Sure Jack, I have plenty of time. How did it go with good old Stan?

Well Jimmy, I didn't jump across his desk and smack him in the face if that's what you're asking.

Laughing on his end, Jimmy added,

That good huh? I commend you Jack O'Brien on your Christian witness in not attacking your boss. Perhaps you should give testimony in church this Sunday!

Very funny Jimmy and I'll keep it in mind. Listen, I know we considered this last night but what about your FBI contact?

Answering, Jimmy said,

I'm ready to go on that. My guy has recently been promoted and is running all the FBI field offices in the metropolitan area. We go way back to high school and over the years we've had several opportunities to work together and share intelligence.

He's a straight-shooter and I think he'll listen to us.

Jack replied,

Very good Jimmy! I'll get off the phone and let you get back to business. Let me know when you've arranged a meeting.

*****

Arriving on the 23rd floor of the Federal Plaza in Manhattan, Jack and Jimmy met for nearly an hour with the FBI's lead agent in the city. Letting Jimmy break the ice and give an overview, Jack then addressed Mike's unusual experiences in greater detail, using the Somali bust as a supporting argument.

Although Jimmy's contact was more cordial and willing to listen than Jack's boss, the outcome proved essentially the same--the political risks of engaging a Christian *mystic* to thwart a potential terror threat to America's most celebrated city were just too astronomical.

Thanking the FBI special agent for his time, they rode the elevator down to street level in silence. Stepping into the lobby together Jimmy was the first to speak.

I'm sorry Jack. I thought we might have had a chance with the FBI but honestly, I understand his reticence to go forward with this.

Nodding his head in agreement Jack replied,

Yeah, it was a swing and a miss and the count is now 0 and two. But the stakes are too high and we need to find someone else who will listen to us.

I am more convinced than ever that Mike's experiences are valid and there is a credible threat looming against this city.

Chapter 60

23 Oct 2017, Bayard Cutting Arboretum, Great River

Mike had gotten the news that neither Jack nor Jimmy was able to convince their DHS or FBI colleagues of a credible threat to New York City. Yet everything inside of her practically screamed danger--heed the warning! She discovered that the only antidote for her inner turmoil was to pray according to the Apostle Paul's instructions to the Corinthian church.

Well then, what shall I do? I shall pray in the spirit, and I will also pray with words I understand.

Having exhausted her own words in prayer she decided to get out of the house and spend time praying in the spirit and in a different setting. Mike knew the beaches would be crowded so instead she drove out to the Bayard Cutting Arboretum in Great River. Traffic was not too bad on the Sunrise Highway and in about forty-five minutes she pulled into an *oasis of beauty and tranquility* nestled beside the lazy Connetquot River.

The Arboretum was created in 1887 and eventually donated to the Long Island State Park Region by Mrs. William Bayard Cutting in loving member of her husband. Mike loved its serenity and the extensive plantings of dwarf evergreens, rhododendron, azaleas, wildflowers, hollies, and oaks.

Although it was October, it was still a lovely place to take a walk with God! Choosing a path that led to the river Mike began her conversation.

Lord, You know the burden of my heart especially as You were the One who caused me to dream and hear what I heard.

But I don't know what else to pray anymore so I'm switching gears. I'm just going to pray in the spirit and let You sort out the details.

So as her senses took in nature's beauty, she also prayed in the language of the Holy Spirit first experienced by the disciples on the Day of Pentecost. Every now and then, she would stop to smell a flower or observe the wind catching the tops of the trees. After a while, she arrived at a small grassy area with an inviting rustic bench that melded into the scenery.

She sat down and became very still and quiet. Some people feared being alone with themselves but not Mike. With all the hustle and bustle of twenty-first century living, she was quite happy not hearing a phone, a cat, motorcycle or even another human voice.

With practiced effort, she sat motionless and soon emptied herself out. Glancing about Mike panned her eyes across the open area, first in one direction and then another. After a second sweep of her surroundings, her attention was drawn towards an ornate metal gate with a "C" embossed on the upper bars. Unwittingly, Mike was about to experience an unusual spiritual event.

Intrigued, she walked over, opened the gate, and then followed a long driveway lined with trees and beautiful flowers. Leaving the shade of the trees, Mike stood looking at a magnificent French Renaissance style mansion with a circular drive leading to an attached five or six car-garage. The garage doors were all closed.

As she approached the house, the front door opened and she walked in without thinking at all whether she had been invited. She then passed one beautifully furnished room after another until arriving at the master bedroom of the house. Mike was certain it was the master bedroom, although she wasn't certain how she knew that. Opening the double doors herself, she saw a tall Caucasian man speaking to a petite Asian woman with beautiful dark flowing hair.

The couple seemed agitated and the man kept gesturing with his hand towards one wall of their bedroom. Right at that moment, a section of the wall slid away and Mike followed the couple as they entered into a much smaller room filled with security screens, computer monitors, a gun rack, and emergency supplies.

The man walked over to a sturdy metal rack in a corner of the room and that is when Mike saw the containers. Peering closely at each one, she realized that she had seen them before...

It was in her dream--they were the same dreadful containers loaded into the submarine!

After seeing the containers, Mike knew it was time to leave. Just before exiting the house, she was drawn to a library positioned at the front of the house and facing the circular drive. She walked in and then over to a beautiful mahogany desk with a single book resting on top of it.

The book was *The Spy*, James Fenimore Cooper's second novel. Flipping to the front page was an inscription,

To Jimbo and Jin Lee,
May this book inspire you to great exploits!

The inscription was left unsigned but it was alright, Mike had seen enough!

And then suddenly, she was once again surrounded by the beauty of the Bayard Cutting Abortorium.

Chapter 61

25 October 2017, Garden City

In great detail, Mike finished sharing what she had seen at the Arboretum with the pastors, the Falso's, and her in-laws. After a round of questions to clarify and fine tune what they had heard, the group began to discuss certain aspects of the open vision they thought were important.

The Hanson's were intrigued by the apparent wealth represented by the house and grounds. Jimmy Falso focused on the embossed "C" on the gate and the fact that the couple had a safe room built into the bedroom. His wife Diane noted that the Asian woman was more likely a North Korean. Jack on the other hand, concentrated on the two containers and wondered what route they had taken from the sub to the couple's mansion. And finally, Gwen was captivated by the last scene in the vision in which Mike visited the library and opened a copy of *The Spy*. Gwen then volunteered,

I read The Spy back in high school and honestly, I don't remember much about it. But I'm going to pick up a copy from the library and reread it. Who knows, something important could surface. And then again, maybe the book's significance has something to do with the couple's first names?

Pastor Kyle jumped in and said,

We really need to continue our praying and expect God to reveal what's important. Each of us thinks we have a piece but the Lord has all the answers.

Then nodding at Mike, Kyle continued.

And let's not forget to keep praying for Mike also. For God's reasons and His alone, He has opened her spiritual eyes and ears to uncover a horrible plot against our country.

Over the years, we've all born witness to her prophetic calling which is a gift seen throughout the Scriptures. King David had Nathan the prophet and Gad the seer to help preserve the kingdom of Israel; the supernatural ministries of Elijah and Elisha not only impacted the children of Israel but the surrounding nations as well; and for those who think women should sit quietly at the back of the church, they need to examine the Old Testament examples of Miriam, Deborah, Isaiah's wife, and Huldah.

The New Testament also mentions the prophetic ministries of Anna and the four daughters of Philip the evangelist as well.

It was then that the Holy Spirit decided to interrupt the pastor's mini-sermon with a message of His own. With a look of glory on her face, Mike lifted her hands to heaven and released what God had just downloaded into her heart.

I am a God of love, forgiveness and mercy and I do not desire the death of any human being. Just as I did with ancient Israel, I have moved in your

21st century to protect your nation from enemy's abroad and enemies within.

Your prayers, and the prayers of My people--not only in this country but in South Korea, China, Pakistan, and even in the Muslim nations of the Middle East, have risen to Me as sweet incense. My Word says that if you would humble yourselves and pray to Me, I would come and heal your land.

That healing wave is coming but I will first demonstrate My power over the nations. I will thwart the plans of the wicked and protect My people.

As Mike sank back into her chair, the word of the Lord brought joy and confidence to everyone in the room. Despite the obstacles they faced, God would not allow evil to prosper.

Chapter 62

The Callahan's considered their trip to Manhattan a scouting success. The parade itself would start on Central Park West and 77th street and continue heading south until reaching Columbus Square. It would then turn east on Central Park South until 6th avenue, where the parade would again head south until it reached 34th street. Arriving at 34th street, the procession would take a quick right towards Macy's Herald Square, and end up at 34th street and 7th avenue.

They chose the Mark New York Hotel on the Upper East Side to place their first nuclear device. It sat just off 77th street on the east side of Central Park. Jin Lee would check into the hotel the night before the parade, leave her *luggage* in the room, and then return to Scarsdale. Using an assumed name, she would pay for a view of the park and insist that she not be disturbed in the morning.

Meanwhile *Jimbo* would place the second bomb in a rented office space on the sixth floor of a building overlooking the Macy's Thanksgiving Day official viewing area on 34th street. The location would be the most crowded along the entire 2.65-mile route and the ensuing carnage would be massive.

They would both use rented vehicles for the drive to the city and for returning to Scarsdale. There was not a concern of a forensic investigation since nothing within a half mile to a mile of either bomb blast would remain standing.

*****

In the days following their trip to the city, Jimbo became increasingly agitated. Jin Lee, as impassive as ever, watched carefully to see where his agitations were taking him. She never let her emotions interfere with assignments but that was not always the case with her husband.

The dam broke the first Saturday morning in November. Sitting by themselves in their informal dining room, *Jimbo* was silent as he pushed his eggs from one side of his plate to the other. Finally, looking up at his wife he said,

Jin Lee, you know what a shock it was when I first found out that you were a North Korean agent. I couldn't believe that as an American intelligence officer I fell in love with an enemy of my country. But I loved you then and I love you now.

Throughout the years we've stolen and passed along documents and information to your government but I've never directly harmed or killed anyone.

Now we're poised to plant two backpack nuclear devices in a city we both learned to enjoy and then walk away as hundreds of thousands, if not

millions of people, lose their lives! You know I never really signed up for something like this.

Suddenly Jin Lee interrupted him and asked,

Then what do you want to do?

Jimbo stared into his wife's eyes and with an unwelcomed realization, he found them hard and unyielding.

I don't know if I can go through with this. We have enough money to make a run for it, pay for new identities, and live off the radar for the rest of lives.

Jin Lee thought for a moment and then replied.

Listen to me very carefully Jimbo Callahan. There is no place safe on the planet for those who fail in their assignments with my countrymen. Death would be around the corner, in the stairwell, or while sitting in your car.

You have but two choices to make. First, you complete this assignment, however unpleasant it is, and continue to live. Or fail in your assignment and sign your own death warrant.

Think about it!

Without another word, Jin Lee got up from the table and walked out of the room.

In watching her leave, *Jimbo* Callahan couldn't shake the feeling that he had married a stranger.

Chapter 63

1 November 2017, White House Press Conference

With a sense of fair play, the White House press secretary acknowledged the hand of a particularly sour critic of the president who worked for one of the six major broadcast network news sites. News about the president's apparently successful stare-down of the North Korean dictator over the ICBM crisis went largely unreported. However, once again attention was being drawn to the president's words--and not his deeds.

Can you tell me why the President hasn't come down harder on some of the radical right-wing factions that have been stirring up racial strife in the country?

Trying not to be caught sighing, the Press Secretary answered.

The President is extremely concerned with the many fractured and even hostile elements in our land. He stated in his inaugural speech that he wanted to make us a great nation again; an inclusive people united in strength and virtue.

Interrupting, the journalist pressed his agenda.

Yes, we've heard all that but what is President Rizzo doing now to stop the spread of bigotry by violent right-wing extremists--the kind that attacks African American churches and supports the covering up of police brutality towards minorities!

Responding, the White House spokesperson said,

I'll answer that but I'm not certain you are willing to really listen.

Bigotry is like a tree with an extensive root system. To uproot it from our culture, we will need the collective efforts of America's churches, our school and university systems, an economic engine and recovery that provides jobs and security to families, and last but certainly not least, we need the same God that helped form this country to come again and teach us how to live with one another.

Standing to his feet, the now irate major media representative began to argue his point; however, the man at the podium simply bypassed him to take a question from a female reporter towards the back of the room.

She began with,

Thank you for taking my question which is really a two-part observation of the president's foreign policies.

First, the North Korean leader has apparently stood down from his bellicose comments and threats over the last couple of months. Secondly,

276

after the president rescinded the controversial Iranian nuclear agreement and reinstituted stronger sanctions, there's been a notable reduction in hostilities on the Israeli and Lebanon border. Finally, Iran's constant flow of inflammatory rhetoric, along with the previous rantings of Pyongyang, has both been muted.

Despite the growing tension in the room, the White House spokesperson forced a smile and added.

I'm sure the President will appreciate your observations. He made a campaign pledge to defend our country from all enemies foreign and domestic. He believes that a strong America is a safer America, not only for our own citizens but for a world community that has had little leadership over the decade.

His belief is that bullies will remain bullies until they meet someone with strength. He intends that the United States of America be a nation that demonstrates strength and virtue to the international community.

Then with a quick *thank you for coming,* he ended the press conference and walked out of the room.

Chapter 64

Jack was in his office busy moving paper from one side of his desk to the other, when Skeeter McCall invited himself in. Skeeter, a strapping six-foot four member of Jack's DHS unit, was a former Navy SEAL and an all-around good guy.

Jack enjoyed Skeeter's company and especially as the guy never seemed to have had a bad day in his life. Of course, that wasn't really the case and he carried scars on his back from an IED in Iraq, a metal plate in his skull where a AK-47 round *nicked* his head, and an history of broken bones, torn ligaments, and one bout with malaria that almost ended his string of *good days*.

Jack thought to himself, *this guy is a tonic to my soul!*

But aside from the positive vibes, Skeeter brought some important news.

Hey Jack, remember when we served on the John F. Kennedy together and Captain D.L. Johnson commanded the ship?

I sure do and to this day he was one of the finest men to ever put on a Navy uniform. I swore back then that I would follow that man into hell itself.

With a brief grin Jack added,

However, I'm not so sure about that going into hell part anymore. Anyway, what about him?

Leaning his big frame towards Jack's desk Skeeter said,

Retired Rear Admiral D.L. Johnson has recently been nominated by the president as the new Deputy Secretary of the DHS! Jack, in a real sense, we will both be working for him again!

For once the folks in Washington got it right!

*****

Jack, Mike, and Jimmy Falso sat patiently in a well-furnished waiting room tucked within the DHS headquarters located on the St. Elizabeth's Hospital campus in Southwest Washington DC. They did not have much of a wait before an aid came and led them through a maze of hallways to the new Deputy Secretary's spacious office.

After introductions, and a bit of nostalgic bantering between two Navy veterans, Secretary Johnson proved a gracious host and an equally good listener. He was also a strong Bible-believing Christian who knew that God was the real strength of the nation.

Then for over an hour, Mike described her three spiritual encounters with Jack and Jimmy jumping in to add their observations to the narrative. At the conclusion, the Secretary shook his head and commented,

That is quite an amazing story but do you have any idea when an attack could possibly be made?

Jack answered,

No sir we don't. We've passed 9/11 on the calendar and the next two major events include Thanksgiving and Christmas. A date is the missing piece of the puzzle.

On the other hand, we've attributed the verbal threats to the man in Pyongyang. The sub transport makes sense if he wanted to avoid commercial transit of what could possibly be backpack nukes to the States. And finally, Mike's vision suggests people with wealth and the prerequisite skills to set up and detonate two bombs in New York City.

Carefully rehearsing Jack's comments, the Secretary asked a question.

Jack, what is it that you want from me?

Sir, Jimmy and I tried to warn both DHS and FBI field offices in the New York metropolitan area. No one, and I'm not offering this as a criticism, wanted to stick their neck out on something like this in the current political climate. Plus, how do you explain Mike's supernatural experiences to secular audiences?

But what I'm asking you for sir is to do some digging within our intelligence systems to try to tie up loose ends. This would enable us to possibly locate the safe house as well as to identify the couple who are likely to still have those containers.

And if our concerns are collaborated, we would want authorization to conduct a raid on the house as soon as possible.

The Secretary considered Jack's comments and said;

Thanks Jack and let me see what I can do. I'm the new guy here I want to check to see whether I'm in calm or stormy waters. But I will get back with you. You can be certain of that!

And Jack, please send my regards to Skeeter for me and tell him I miss his eternal optimism.

And then nodding towards the large bay widow facing the capital he added,

We could use a lot more of that in Washington. That's for sure!

Chapter 65

I t had been three days since their meeting with Deputy Secretary Johnson and the clock was ticking. Everyone was feeling the pressure. And it was Mike that first decided to add fasting to her prayers; an idea which quickly caught on with the rest of the group. Although no one was fully aware of what was taking place in spiritual places, they knew that desperate times required a deeper level of seeking.

When Judah's King Jehoshaphat faced invasion and impossible odds, he proclaimed a fast throughout the land and then set himself to pray and seek the Lord with his whole heart. God responded in a remarkable way giving the king and his people a message for future generations.

Do not be afraid or dismayed because of this multitude, for the battle is not yours, but God's.

Position yourselves, stand still and see the salvation of God.

*****

After they had prayed that evening, Gwen offhandedly mentioned that she finished reading *The Spy*.

You know if we weren't faced with all of this, I would recommend that everyone read it. It's quite good and the plot involved a common man who was accused of being a British spy during the American Revolution.

The author chose the colonial town of Scarsdale for the setting due to the many historic activities that took place in and around the town.

Jack and I traveled through Scarsdale a few years ago and today it is one of the most affluent cities in the country and full of mansions...

Like a huge magnet, the word *mansions* drew everyone's attention. Looking around the room Gwen finally got it too! With a sudden rush of adrenalin, she blurted out.

Scarsdale, wealthy homes, beautiful mansions--and spies!

*****

The next morning Jack received his highly anticipated call from Secretary Johnson.

Hello Jack and I'm sorry it took this long to get back with you but I have some very interesting information for you. Can you drive down to the Capital today?

Yes sir! I would be glad too. Should I bring my daughter-in-law and Captain Falso along with me?

I'm afraid not Jack. I checked and neither one has a top-secret clearance. Attempting to cushion the disappointment he heard in Jack's voice the Secretary added,

We simply don't have enough time for that now. Just come on down as soon as you can.

Jack knew the department's Number Two man was right.

I understand sir and before I get off the phone I believe we've unlocked another piece of the puzzle. We've been praying and fasting and last night, we think we know where the safe house is.

And without waiting for the Secretary's response Jack continued.

It's Scarsdale, up in Winchester County, New York.

There was a long silence on the other end of the line and finally, Secretary Johnson asked,

How did you find out?

A little puzzled by the question, Jack responded.

Well sir, I just told you we've been fasting and praying and…

Cutting him short, the Secretary tried to suppress the excitement in his own voice.

Yes Jack, I heard you and I can't go into details over the phone but let me say this, we're in agreement!

*****

Seated around the Secretary's small conference table were some heavy hitters from the FBI, CIA, and the Defense Intelligence Agency or DIA. Jack was a little uncomfortable with all the brass, but he had utter confidence in Secretary Johnson.

The DIA kicked off the briefing.

Agent O'Brien I want to first commend you for your efforts to prevent an attack on our nation.

I appreciate that sir but I wouldn't be here unless God had used my daughter-in-law to see and hear things that the rest of us couldn't figure out.

The DIA man continued,

At any rate in coordination with the CIA we've been busy tracking North Korea's progress in the development of a new ultra-quiet attack sub. Unfortunately for the regime, we've been on to them for some time and using technology that I am unprepared to disclose, we found a way to tag their newest submarine force.

In late September one of these subs crossed the Pacific and sat quietly off the California coast near San Francisco for two days, probably wanting to make sure it hadn't been noticed.

On day three, the Coast Guard stood off while tracking a forty-foot cabin cruiser which traveled to the same location of our sub. We assumed that the sub and cruiser were there for a reason and we began monitoring the activities of the two boat owners, who happened to be two Koreans working in Silicon Valley.

And at this point, my CIA colleague will finish the narrative.

Speaking from the other side of the table, the CIA rep added,

We had our eyes on the Koreans who are employees of Fail-Safe Computer Solutions; a company that we discovered has deeply buried ties to Pyongyang. To cut to the chase, the Koreans in question decided to take a cross-country business trip with a rented vehicle. We managed to get to it beforehand and conceal our own miniature GPS tracker.

Now smiling the CIA presenter continued,

And you'll never guess where our two gentlemen stopped for a night?

At that point, Jack got it and smiling back at the intelligence operator, he replied.

Let me guess? Scarsdale?

You're right on the money Agent O'Brien. Right on the money!

The FBI agent finished up by providing the full names of the two prime suspects. James *Jimbo* Callahan and his Korean wife Jin Lee did indeed live in a palatial home in Scarsdale's exclusive Murray Hill-Heathcote neighborhood--and they had a front gate featuring an embossed "C" on it. He had been a former Air Force intelligence officer and Jin Lee's background was sketchy at best.

Looking around the table, Deputy Secretary Johnson thanked everyone for their contributions. Then turning to the FBI special agent, he asked,

Do we need to go through the courts and get a warrant?

The agent replied,

Due to the nature of this threat and the evidence in hand, we can get a fast track warrant and be ready to go in twenty-four hours.

Deputy Secretary Johnson ended the meeting with a few parting words.

Very good gentlemen! I know you'll need to brief your superiors and I will do the necessary coordination at my level.

Keep me posted on the outcome of the raid and let's hope and pray that we find what we expect to find in Scarsdale.

With an ear-to-ear grin, Jack shook the hand of his old commanding officer and said, *I can't thank you enough sir.*

Chapter 66

It was four-thirty in the morning and the FBI's special countermeasures van sat a hundred yards along the small access road which ran to the Callahan's massive front gate. Those inside the cramped interior would use the latest technology to listen in on conversations and put out the electronic eyes of the estate's security system. Another team of FBI cyber experts tapped into the couple's wireless system and phones.

Outside the walls and front entrance to the mansion, the grim-faced members of an Enhanced FBI SWAT team moved into position. The Enhanced Team was larger than most SWAT teams and they had access to a more extensive range of tactical equipment and methods.

The watch words of the morning would be stealth, speed, shock and awe! The time to burst through the front and rear entrances, toss in their stun grenades and enter the Callahan's bedroom would be less than twenty seconds.

The hour of the morning, the flash and bang grenades, and the speed of the swarming SWAT members would usually do the trick for most raids. But Jin Lee was no ordinary suspect!

Hearing the front door crashed open, Jin Lee instantly reacted to her years of training. Deftly she rolled out of bed, grabbed a CZ PO9 handgun with a twenty-round clip, and buried her face and head under a pillow as the first of two stun grenades were tossed into the room.

Jimbo awoke in a panic and started shouting until the first grenade temporarily blinded him by activating all the photoreceptor cells in his eyes. At the same time the blast shut down his auditory system causing him to fall disoriented to the floor.

And then a second grenade was tossed in for insurance!

Jin Lee knew what to expect and she kept her head face down on the bed. Shortly afterwards, the first agent ducked the room and took a 9-millimeter round in the leg which threw him to the ground gritting in pain. A second member of the SWAT team was more fortunate barely escaping a volley of bullets passing within inches of his head. Though she was outgunned, Jin Lee was determined to go down fighting.

She didn't have long to wait as shards of glass exploded into the room revealing a gaping hole in the wall where two French Doors had previously been. Agents pouring into the room created just enough of a distraction to cause the North Korean operative to change stances and briefly expose her position. An intense firefight ensued with a withering crossfire laid down by tactical units moving in from the patio and hallway.

After over a hundred rounds had been fired at the target, the on-scene commander shouted *clear!* The only sounds in the room were those of a prone and whimpering *Jimbo* Callahan, who kept repeating,

Don't shoot! Don't shoot I am unarmed!

Immediately agents advanced on Jin Lee's unmoving body and secured the handgun lying near her outstretched hand. Her husband stood to his feet and his wrists were bound with elastic bands. His eyes streamed with tears as he fixed his gaze on his wife's crumpled body. Without much coaxing, he led agents into the couple's safe room and directly to the backpack nukes still housed in their special containers.

After the team had secured the crime scene, the on-scene commander radioed in that the mission had been a success and the entire contingency planning team breathed a sigh of relief. Later that day, Jack O'Brien would receive a personal phone call from retired Rear Admiral Johnson.

The threat to America's most prominent city had been thwarted...at least for the time being.

Chapter 67

Arising before his normal waking hour, North Korean's tyrant eagerly anticipated an unprecedented day of vengeance lavished upon America's Great Apple. Though he loved so many facets of American life, including the great game of basketball, the U.S. had remained a major thorn in his family's budding dynasty. Moreover, he positively loathed the pretentious ranting of its chief executive, who he was certain had authorized the unsuccessful hit on his motorcade.

At five-foot seven, Kin Gun Suk's weight had ballooned to nearly three hundred pounds--a weight some sources had claimed led to fractured ankles. Despite his wobbly gait, he walked to the center of his enormously large and empty bedroom suite, and spoke to the gods of the air.

We shall soon see how boisterous this Rizzo is when his precious New York City is filled with a radioactive cloud that will linger for centuries. This is a day when dreams come true and America's financial center will become a no-man's land.

Immensely pleased with himself, he spoke into a hand-held device and ordered his usual huge breakfast.

I want my regular breakfast in fifteen minutes and not a minute later. Then with a spark of inspiration he added,

And bring me a large piece of New York cheesecake. I warn you it must be a New York cheesecake and not anything else.

*****

It was eight in the morning, a full hour before New York's world-famous Thanksgiving parade would kick off. The President had summoned a few key staff and cabinet members to the Situation Room in the West Wing. Banquet tables had been set up and at nine a.m., the White House kitchen staff would fill the room with all the trimmings of a traditional Thanksgiving meal.

The meeting was not a war council nor was it a policy making event. Great matters affecting the Republic would be temporarily set aside. Instead a profoundly thankful President purposed to celebrate the holiday with the people who walked with him through the recent stormy seas.

Although the incident would be buried in history's secret vault, the men and women in the room knew the Almighty had revealed the plot of a madman and in so doing, He spared the nation from an unprecedented catastrophe. Throughout history, God used men and women to hear His voice and to

294

reveal what heaven wanted them to see for His purposes. God spoke to the prophet Jeremiah and said,

See, I have this day set you over the nations and over the kingdoms, to root out and pull down, to destroy and throw down, to build and to plant.

Before filling Isaiah's mouth with messages from above, God first allowed him a vision of heaven. The experience of seeing God utterly changed his life and he influenced kings and kingdoms for his Lord and Master.

And through the faithful obedience of a chosen handmaiden, He protected a modern metropolis of nearly nine million. But God was not finished…there was a nation to heal, a president to lead, and a dictator to deal with.

*****

Fourteen and a half hours ahead of New York City, North Korea's leader gathered a select group of *yes-men* to the Kumsusan Palace of the Sun, situated on the northeast corner of the capital city. Constructed in 1976 at an estimated cost of nearly one billion dollars, the palace also doubled as a mausoleum for Kim Gun Suk's father and grandfather.

Oddly enough, with Pyongyang a full fourteen and a half hours ahead of the East Coast, the Great Leader would view the destruction of New York City on the 24th of November. But it didn't matter. The weapons of mass destruction would detonate precisely at nine a.m. as the 91st annual Macy's Thanksgiving Parade began filling the city's streets with its world-famous helium balloons and floats.

With the large World Clock in the room set to 9 a.m. Eastern Standard Time, Kim and his uniformed *guests* sat around a large semi-circular table. In an expansive mood, the dictator had food, beverages, and even fine wines on hand for the spectacle. A large screen that ran nearly the length of the room was streaming NBC's coverage of the event along with running commentary by the station's talking heads.

The clock kept ticking off the minutes: fifteen, twelve, ten, eight, and then five. The atmosphere was thick with an excitement seasoned with an adrenalin rush quite often felt by high wire trapeze artists.

The countdown continued: four minutes, three, two, and then one. Seconds mattered now and every eye was riveted on the screen stretched out before them. As the last second touched home base, the parade kicked off with hundreds of thousands of people lined along the parade's route.

The clock now read 9:01 and then 9:02 and still all was calm in the city targeted for destruction. The minutes kept marching by until everyone in the room knew that something had gone terribly wrong. With every eye riveted on their stone-faced leader, not a soul moved in their chair and no one offered an explanation.

At 9:30, Kim Gun Suk suddenly stood up and without a word, walked out of the room. In his darkened heart, he knew the plot had failed but he was confident the Americans would implicate the Iranians. After all, he had been outfoxing the world for years.

Later that day, and still smarting from the failed attempt, he received an official diplomatic pouch personally delivered to him from a high official in the United Kingdom's embassy. This was highly unusual but the UK representative insisted that it was for the Great Leader's eyes only.

After having the pouch scanned and examined for chemical compounds, Kim Gun Suk took the correspondence into his study and sat down at his desk. Deftly using a gold-plated letter opener, he reached into the sealed mailbag and removed a letter housed in another sealed envelope.

Unfolding the letter, the Great Leader's hands began to tremble for at the top of the page was the seal of the President of the United States. Below the seal were just two printed words.

WE KNOW!

And now, Kim Gun Suk knew also!

Chapter 68

1 December 2017, White House

Mike carefully took in her surroundings half believing that in a few minutes she would meet the president of the United States in the Oval Office. Sitting beside her was her father-in-law Jack O'Brien and Jimmy Falso, cheerful as ever in his finest police dress uniform. Although they both appeared calm, Mike was nervous and feeling embarrassed from all the attention they had been receiving from the White House staff.

As for the spoiled plot, for reasons of national security, federal agents had cordoned off the story and the incident never surfaced in newspaper headlines or prime time talk shows. Thanksgiving Day 2017 would be remembered for its parades, football games, and too many calories. To be certain, millions of lives would never know how close to their Maker they had come or the fact, that it was indeed their Maker who had graciously spared them!

Yet in a short time, the man who was at the helm of the nation would know everything.

*****

The unsung heroes did not have long to wait before the door opened and an aid waved them into the nation's most famous office. Standing to greet them was the president, followed by the vice president, Secretaries of State and Defense, the Attorney General, National Security Advisor, and the newly minted White House Chief of Staff.

President Rizzo warmly welcomed each of them and in turning to Mike he said,

And you must be Michelina O'Brien!

Yes Mr. President and if you please sir, I'm Mike. That's what my family and friends call me.

Her response launched a presidential smile.

Well, then Mike I'm awfully proud to meet you as well as the rest of your home-spun anti-terror team.

Quick introductions were made around the room and afterwards the President motioned for Mike, Jack, and Jimmy to be seated.

On behalf of a nation that will almost certainly never know what you did for it, I want to thank you and express my personal gratitude for

thwarting a catastrophic attack on the city and its residents who are very dear to me.

What you did in alerting local authorities and our intelligence agencies was in the finest tradition of the men and women who by faith founded and helped to defend this great nation.

Then focusing his attention on Mike, he continued.

I understand Mike that you had a significant role in seeing and hearing the plans of these enemies without ever leaving Long Island.

In a quiet voice Mike responded,

Sir, let me be perfectly clear that without the help of my father-in-law and Captain Falso I would not have been able to contact the right people to stop the attack.

More importantly, I am a mother, a businesswoman, and a Christian lady who knows nothing about backpack nuclear devices, intelligence capabilities or geopolitical considerations. It was God who peeled back a layer of the supernatural to reveal the plot in all its wicked design. He allowed me to hear the North Korean leader's words. He let me see the backpacks in transit and then see the safe house in Scarsdale.

It was God at the helm the entire time!

I cannot tell you Mr. President why the Lord God selected me to see and hear things in the spiritual realm. But He did and because of His merciful love for people--and for this great nation, He stopped a wicked plan by using a quite ordinary human vessel.

Visibly affected by what he had heard, Matthew Rizzo sat back in his chair, bowed his head, and then asked the Vice President to lead those in attendance in a prayer of thanksgiving.

With tears streaming down his face, Sam Blackstone prayed as if there were no one else in the room.

Dear heavenly Father, on a day we celebrate a national Day of Thanksgiving, You stopped the hand of the wicked from causing great harm to our land. Once again, You showered us with rich and undeserved mercy for we have become a people in danger of forgetting their God.

Continue Your loving-kindness and grant us repentance and forgiveness through the Blood of Your Son Jesus. Heal our hearts and make us one united nation under God again.

And Father, please grant everyone in this office the strength to do what is right in Your sight. Amen.

As the Vice President concluded, it occurred to Mike that the Oval Office had become an Oval Chapel! The presence of God was thick in the room as leaders of the mightiest nation on earth yielded their hearts to a greater sovereign power.

It was simply awesome!

After kneeling beside his desk, the president then stood up and moved in front of his three guests.

Jack, Jimmy, thank you again for your tenacity and invaluable contributions in thwarting this terrible plot against our land.

Then turning to Mike, he added,

And Mike I know you have a very busy life with your children, business, and ministry but I have a special deal for you that will add a little something else to your plate.

With a questioning look Mike responded,

What kind of a deal Mr. President? What are you adding to my plate?

Flashing an ear to ear grin, the nation's chief executive explained,

Well Mike it seems to me that our National Security Council could use a little help every now and then. That's why I've volunteered you as a Special Advisor to the NSA!

Congratulations! I know you'll do a great job!

Then beginning with the President, everyone in the room began to clap and congratulate Mike on her *new position!* Amused by the stunned look on Mike's face, Jimmy Falso gave her a well-deserved hug and quipped,

That's how the man makes deals Mike! Just like that!

After several minutes, the same aid who had escorted the trio into the Oval Office led them to the West Wing's lobby. As they waited for transportation, each marveled at the sovereign works of a God who ruled the heavens and the earth!

Epilogue

Please note that in all but a few cases, the outcome of our story ends on a positive note. Those exceptions of course include Jin Lee, who paid the ultimate price for her espionage against the U.S.; *Jimbo* Callahan, who despite full cooperation with Federal agents, would spend the rest of his natural life in a maximum-security prison; and finally, the extremely paranoid leader of the People's Democratic Republic of Korea who was given good reason to worry about his future.

In a flip of the coin, the Big Apple and its millions of residents were spared an unthinkable nuclear disaster, the likes of which would have redefined the word *horrific!* Captain Jimmy Falso was cited for his efforts and promoted to Deputy Inspector in an expanded anti-terrorism unit intent on developing closer ties with the DHS.

As for Jack O'Brien well...remember Stan Hanover? He <u>had</u> <u>been</u> Jack's boss and was quite unwilling to take a career risk when made aware of a potential threat to nearly nine million people! That didn't go over well with the new DHS Deputy Secretary who found a nice quiet desk job for Stan deep in the bowels of a departmental building in Washington DC. Then to the delight of all who worked with him, Jack was promoted to Stan's position in charge of all the DHS field offices in the greater New York City metropolitan area. Of course, Jack hadn't changed his plans to hang up his spurs the following year--but for the time being it was good to be the boss!

Not to be left out, both wives benefited in other ways such as Tracey's long-awaited vacation to the Caribbean and Gwen's shiny new 2018 Subaru Forester sitting in her driveway. The Hansen's received an official Letter of Commendation from the White House plus a special presidential offer to pay the church a visit. The topic of discussion: Prayers that affect government.

And finally, we come to Mike, a woman who had no greater ambition than to walk humbly before God, grow old with her husband, and be a mother to her children. But life took a painful fork in the road and there would be no husband at her side.

Instead God came closer.

He always does when it's darkest.

And so, Mike would continue to live, learn, and love while honoring God with the gifts she had received. Would the White House give her a call?

It's possible you will find the answer to that question on another page and in another book.

Acknowledgements

A special thanks to Pina, my faithful editor and critic, who has walked many pages and word counts with me while supplying much needed encouragement and advice.

I also appreciate Elsa and Mike for their feedback, inspiration and shared passion for coffee.

And finally, to the Gift-Giver Himself who makes all things possible—and beautiful at the same time.

Made in the USA
Columbia, SC
15 August 2018